CTJ Reeves: Asmeron

Auth

I have never considered mys_____ive, so I was pleasantly surprised to find I had an unusual story inside of me. Asmeron is my debut novel.

Copyright ©2016

CTJ Reeves: Asmeron

For Todd and Joel

I would like to acknowledge my friend Sue Storey whose contribution has been invaluable.

ASMERON

In the not too distant future!!

CHAPTER: ONE

They did it, they actually did it. Stupid - Stupid – Bastards! Everywhere around me is totally devastated. The sky has turned into a paralysing, unnatural, blinding white, as if a blanket of heavy snow is above me instead of beneath me. Large clouds of black, acrid smoke are rising into the sky forcing it to become darker and darker. The whole world will soon be in a perpetual twilight. The force of a tornado like wind is throwing burning debris high into the air and as far as my eyes can see there are flames, turning the sky above me and the ground around me into a blazing inferno - Hell on Earth.

Large burning trees are being uprooted from the ground as though they were nothing more than saplings, being catapulted through the hellish sky like glowing, burning arrows. Fireballs are everywhere with the wreckage of the surrounding neighbourhood raining down from the sky, including parts of my neighbours' homes and cars, exploding into flames once they make impact with the ground.

The window in front of me suddenly explodes, simultaneously, everything crumbles all around me. The floor has collapsed beneath me as I plummet downwards with the rubble of my home pounding down on top of me. I must lose consciousness for a time because the next thing I realise is that I'm lying on the floor of the cellar underneath this old house, half buried in the rubble. The house has been completely destroyed. All I can see are the clouds of black, acrid smoke above me, I'm shrouded in darkness and it's now eerily silent. How on earth have I survived that? How am I still in one piece? Am I still in one piece?

I know my left arm is definitely broken as I can see white bone protruding through my skin. My right arm amazingly seems intact, so I'm able to start dislodging the smaller pieces of rubble within reach. As I'm pushing the rubble away from me I can feel heat radiating from the ground. I'm terrified as I think I'm about to become a human fireball. I'm frantically trying to clear the rubble but I know this is futile as there is too much and it's just too heavy, I can't do anymore. This is it, I'm as good as dead, I'm not in excruciating pain and hopefully soon I will be with my son.

CTJ Reeves: Asmeron

Normal wars were no longer good enough, didn't do enough harm, everyone's gone nuclear. All the super powers, both old and new have finally pressed their 'red buttons' ... 3-2-1... The world I know has been obliterated... IT'S OVER!

The clouds of black smoke start drifting towards me, I can't escape it as any movement now makes it difficult to breathe. Lack of oxygen must be making me hallucinate because I can see two or three shapes moving towards me. Maybe it's not a hallucination after all as the nearer the shapes get to me, the more it becomes clear they are actually people wearing what look like luminous silver hazmat suits. I try to attract their attention by making one final effort to move. As I try and call out the smoke rushes in and fills my lungs and everything goes black.

The next time I open my eyes, I find myself in a brilliantly lit room lying on a bed covered by a thin sheet. The light is so bright it's painful so I pull the sheet up over my head to shield my eyes. In doing this I realise I can move my left arm and I can't feel any pain. I reach over to check if it's still broken but I can't feel a bone sticking out. My whole body is covered in some sort of strange material. It feels ultra thin, like a fine, soft, grey paper tissue. It appears to be seamless and is moulded to every part of me. When I move, it moves, so it's flexible and feels comfortable. I'm completely covered, including my head. The only exposed areas are my eyes, nose and mouth but they feel as though they have been treated with some sort of lubricant or gel.

I can only think I must have been badly burned and this is some sort of new technology to help me heal. Beneath this covering I can feel I'm also wearing some sort of collar around my neck. It feels about half an inch thick and seems to be fixed in place. It's more solid than the material, maybe some sort of ultra thin metal, I can feel fine lines etched into this metal at the front of the collar, some of these lines feel thicker than others, this whole etching spans approximately three inches at the front with the rest being completely smooth. I feel around the sides of the collar and I'm almost certain that at both sides of my neck it's actually going through my skin. Like the unusual body wrap I can't get it off, it isn't causing me any physical pain or major discomfort, I just don't understand what it is, what's going on or why I'm here and I'm too scared to try and move anymore.

No-one and I mean no-one, could have survived the fallout of the bombs, yet here I am, I'm still breathing, my eyes are open and my mind is still functioning. I remain frozen with the sheet pulled over my head for what seems like a very long time as the room stays unnaturally brightly lit. I think I can hear a sound, I'm not sure; I think it could be the sound of breathing. God I hope I'm right! The not knowing is driving me insane so

CTJ Reeves: Asmeron

I decide I've got to try and move, sit up and take in my surroundings, I have to try and figure out what is going on.

Slowly I check everything is working and then I manoeuvre myself into a sitting position. As the sheet falls away I have to quickly close my eyes to allow them to adjust to the brightness. After a few seconds I try opening them again and I can't believe what I'm seeing, there are an unbelievable amount of metal beds. The room looks like a very large dormitory; it's still uncomfortably bright and I have to use one of my hands to shield my eyes, this allows me to scan the room and I can see a sheet, similar to mine, covering a shape lying in each bed, but I can't see any movement from any one of them.

There are no visible light fittings or light switches of any sort to be seen on the walls or the ceiling so the lighting must be controlled from outside of this room. The room is rectangular in shape, with two extremely long walls and two shorter ones at either end. There are no windows but there are two doors. One door is on the shorter wall at the far end of the room to the right and the other door is in the middle of the long wall on the left-hand side, not too far away from my bed. I can't see a door handle or any means of opening it from inside this room. Apart from the two doors and the endless rows of beds, there is absolutely nothing else visible.

CTJ Reeves: Asmeron

Maybe I'm in some sort of hospital, where everyone in this room has survived. Or, I've actually died and I'm at some gateway in the Universe. I have no idea what is going on and I desperately need to talk to someone.

I need to find out who is in those beds. As terrified as I am; I force myself to go and look. I tentatively move my legs from off the bed to the floor and using the bed for support, I find I'm able to stand. Even though I seem to be the only one awake, I feel self-conscious and wrap the sheet around me before I investigate. The sheet is the same light grey colour as the body wrap and feels as light as a feather. Thankfully, I'm mobile, just a little unsteady but I'm not in any physical pain.

There are two rows of beds opposite each other towards the centre of the room with the foot of each bed facing each other; this leaves a wide corridor like space round the outside of the room, almost like a race track. At a glance I think there could be seventy to ninety beds. I decide to manoeuvre myself along each row, holding onto each bed as I go. I'm not sure how long it takes me but I feel completely drained and exhausted by the time I get back to my own bed. I counted eighty beds, including mine, and under the cover on each bed there is a young woman. The beds appear to be made from a single piece of silvery grey metal and there are no mattresses or pillows on any of the beds.

Each woman is lying motionless and has been placed in a full body wrap and each woman has a collar around their neck, the same as me. The collar is a silver colour, more or less half an inch thick and there are tiny lines etched into the metal at the front, the same as mine. From what I can see the lines on each of the women's collars differ slightly, it's like we have all been bar-coded.

As I get back into my own bed I can feel that the metal I have been lying on is rock-hard but, as I lie down it feels as though it has moulded itself around my body and is extremely comfortable. I'm now totally confused and it has really scared me seeing these unconscious women. I'm unable to make sense of what I've just seen as exhaustion takes over and I fall back into a deep sleep.

When I next wake, I can see there is some kind of tunic like garment at the bottom of my bed. This tunic is a mix of silver and grey in colour; it feels paper thin and soft to the touch. Because the material is so thin, I expect it to be transparent, it isn't. I hold it against me and it looks as though it will cover my body from underneath the collar around my neck to just above my knees. Seeing this tunic has made me feel very uneasy. Someone must have seen me wrap the sheet around me when I went to investigate. Does this mean we are all being watched and monitored? If that's the case, why didn't someone come to talk to me when they saw I was awake? I know someone is watching us all, I just don't know who or why!

I'm sure I can hear crying, it sounds as though it's coming from the far end of the room. I want to go and find out who it is so I pull the tunic over the body wrap, as there is no way of removing either it or the collar around my neck. As I look up, the woman in the bed directly opposite to me is sitting upright just mutely staring at me. As we continue to just stare at each other, some of the other women begin to sit up and turn; they all seem to be focusing on me. Seeing so many women trussed up like 'mummies' is surreal. We are all just staring at each other in silence. One of us has got to speak, so I decide to introduce myself: *"Hi, my name is Allie, does anyone have any idea what's happening here? Does anyone know where we are?"*

My voice sounds slightly muffled but coherent. I spoke louder than I normally would have to make sure I was heard, but no one has responded. Maybe they didn't hear me after all, I'm starting to think this is all in my imagination and I've gone totally insane, when two of the women nearest to me call out: *"Hi, I'm Sal, I've no idea where we are or what's happening."*

"I'm Jess, no ideas here either."

The other women start to call out their names. I can hear Irina, Simone, Mattie and a whole host of others. Then the woman in the bed opposite looks directly at me, tells me her name is Bea and asks: *"Do you think we could be in a hospital?"*

"We could be but if someone is treating us, making us well, I don't understand why no-one has come to see us and explain what damage has been done. Maybe if we compare what each of us remembers we might be able to piece together some of this jigsaw puzzle."

We take turns recounting our last memories. We all remember seeing the sky turn into an unnatural, blinding white, swiftly followed by black smoke, turning day into night with a suddenness that was frightening. We all heard the sound of a tornado like wind, travelling at an incredible speed, which was hurling burning debris into the air and spreading fireballs everywhere. Also, I'm not the only one to have seen the figures in the hazmat suits. None of us are in any physical pain and we all agree the body wrap we are wearing could be due to severe burns and broken bones, but no-one has any idea why we are wearing a collar around our neck.

Whilst we are talking the quality of the air changes and seems to feel heavier somehow; making us all start to feel drowsy. We all lie back down on our beds and, as one, we fall asleep.

·······

"Have they all been sedated?"

"Yes."

"How do you wish to proceed?"

"Take the two women that regained consciousness first, the one called Allie and the one called Bea. We need to examine them again and check their mental activity against our earlier results to see if there are any anomalies and also check their healing sheaths to see if the skin grafts have been successful and if their bodies are physically stronger in some way."

"Soon they will all start to get restless. They will have many questions."

"I am aware of that and some of those questions we will be unable to answer at this point in time. Our first priority must be their physical healing."

"Our monitors show the level of radiation is rapidly decreasing."

"Good, we can now progress to the second phase of recovery. All the healing sheaths can be removed. The lighting needs to be adjusted to stimulate the next stage of their physical healing. The lower halves of their bodies were damaged the most, so we need to concentrate more on those areas and continue monitoring closely.

We already know that humans are able to adapt and learn. They are also capable of processing logic, rational thought and to some extent control. I am intrigued by the behaviour of these women. I think they may be more judicious than we first thought. We know there is a defect with one of the women and we may find a few more may be unsuitable, but in general and considering the circumstances we have chosen well.

When we meet them in person we will let them know that we are neither humans nor aliens but we need to understand them more before we present ourselves to them and explain why they are here.

It is the duty of all of us to implement the plans of the Researchers. They transferred to us all the data of their life's work and it is up to us to carry this through to completion."

....

I don't know how long I've been asleep for but there appears to have been some changes. The room is no longer unbearably bright and the temperature is far more comfortable. The moulded body wrap has been removed and I'm completely naked but I'm still wearing a collar around my neck. I move my hands over my body and everything is still where it should be, but as I feel over the top of my arms something feels different. At the top of my left arm I'm sure I can feel something under the skin, it feels as though there are two miniature sized ingots inside my arm. I can feel myself start to freak out as I don't know what the hell is happening to me.

I know I must have been badly burned, yet the skin on my whole body appears to be new. I must have had a skin graft of some sort as my skin is completely free of any crease, mark or scar. I'm completely hair free; there is no hair on my legs, under my arms or any other part of my body. I rub my hands over my head, nothing. I'm completely bald and I can feel myself start to panic. After everything I've been through since the 'war to end all wars', I'm upset because I have no bloody hair, how stupid is that!

I've just realised something else, which is far more important. I don't know exactly how long we've all been here but it has definitely been long enough to know we need to eat and drink. I can't remember being hungry or thirsty since I woke up in this room and that is definitely not normal. How can any of us still be alive without any form of sustenance?

I'm so grateful I'm not on my own here as I desperately need to speak to someone. I sit up and pull the sheet up to cover my nakedness and look up and down the room. I can see one other person sat up; it's the one who introduced herself as Sal. I wave and call out: *"Are you still wearing a body wrap?"*

"No."

"What does your skin look like?"

"It doesn't look like it's been burned or anything and I can't see or feel any hair on my body."

"Can you feel something under the skin at the top of one of your arms?"

"Yes, my left one, it's really freaking me out as I don't know what it is."

"Is there a collar still stuck around your neck?"

"Yes, that's also freaking me out, what the hell is going on? I take it it's the same for you?"

"Yes."

"Allie, it's Jess, it's the same for me too."

Then almost immediately, other women start to join in and there is a chorus of *"me too"*, *"me too"* *"and me."*

Then the one who introduced herself as Bea says: *"Instead of shouting out to each other we need to get together and try and work out what is going on."*

We all cover ourselves with the tunics, the women furthest away get out of their beds and make their way to where the rest of us have congregated. I perch on the end of my bed as others gather round. As I look at everyone I can see what a mixed bunch we all are, not just in age but ethnicity, some look very young, late teen's maybe? The majority of the women look as though they're in their early to mid twenties, there are others who look older, thirties maybe? Sal looks young, Jess looks a similar age to me and Bea looks to be one of the oldest.

As we continue to talk about ourselves it soon becomes apparent that many of us are from different countries. I tell them I'm from England and find out Sal's from Ireland and Jess is from America, the Deep South, but Bea says she's from Russia. I compliment her on her English and she tells me she's not speaking English, she's speaking Russian! Some of the other women then say they are speaking in their own native language and yet I can understand everything everyone is saying and everyone can understand me. Jess must be thinking the same thing as she says: *"Less than half of us are from English speaking countries, yet we can all understand each other, I don't understand how this is possible."*

I quickly answer this one: *"The one thing they've left on each of us is the collar around our necks. They remind me of some sort of bar-code and I'm convinced these have something to do with us all being able to communicate with each other. How on earth this is even possible I've no idea. I'm just hoping someone will start to explain things to us soon; especially where we are and what's happened to us and the rest of the human race."*

Sal speaks next: *"What the hell have they put in my arm and why haven't I got any hair?*

A woman called Chi explains she's a doctor and says: *"Judging by everyone's recollections, it seems we have survived some kind of nuclear explosion. If we have, then there's a good chance that the loss of our hair is due to radiation from the fallout of the bombs and it may still be in our system. This is not my field of expertise, so I do not know if our hair loss will be permanent or not. We all appear to have two small implants under the skin on our left arm. Like the rest of you; I don't know why they have done this"*

Bea joins in: *"Someone seems to be going to an awful lot of trouble to repair us and keep us alive. All we need now is to understand who and why!"*

We are all at a complete loss as to where we are, how we got here, what's happening to us and why. We continue to talk to each other about our lives; the youngest ones here are called Sal, Mattie and Sameena. They say they were in their last year at school; those who are a little older were at Uni. Some of the women were mothers and preferred to work part-time; some were single parents, like me, some of the women were in full-time employment; others were struggling to find any employment at all. There are a few career women amongst us, a few teachers and three doctors. The doctors introduce themselves as Lucy, who is an orthopaedic surgeon, Chi, who is a neurosurgeon, and Jenna, who is a psychiatrist. We appear to come from all walks of life.

I'm hoping we won't need the services of Dr Lucy or Dr Chi, but Dr Jenna could be in demand. The majority of the women are distraught and desperate to know what's happened to their family and friends. Others, like me, have no-one; as everyone they loved has already died. Listening to them talk about their loved ones, the pain in their voices is nearly too much to bear. Suddenly, out of nowhere, comes a crackling sound, then a voice:

"**Attention, Attention.**"

We all completely freeze in disbelief; a strange sounding voice from nowhere has really unnerved each and every one of us.

"**Your bodies are healing rapidly but there is still a slight amount of residual radiation within your system, this is why this is only a verbal communication. We have repaired your damaged skin by using our advanced** *biomaterial technology which includes numerous minuscule layers of ultrathin coatings which resemble what your doctors may know as nanosheets and using your own DNA. We have the ability to speak different languages but not all of them; the collar around your neck will help us to communicate with you and enables you to communicate with each other. The Researchers on the dwarf planet in your solar system called Ceres spoke many languages, but the chosen international language is English and this is the language I am using now.*

Considering the extent of your injuries when we first brought you here, your recovery is progressing faster than we had anticipated. I appreciate you must all have a lot of questions and when we meet in person I will endeavour to answer those I can. What I will say to you is; providing you do not become destructive or dangerous, no harm will come to you. If any of us had wanted to harm you, you would have been left amongst the other nine billion humans, who were burnt beyond recognition, damaged beyond repair or dead."

We hear a slight crackling sound again, then nothing! The room becomes silent. I am trying to make sense of what has just happened, when some of the women start to randomly shout out:

CTJ Reeves: Asmeron

"Who or what the fuck was that!"

"Whoever or whatever it is, we are definitely being watched."

"Did anyone make any sense of what was being said?"

"Nine billion people damaged or dead!" If we are not destructive, no harm will come to us - what the bloody hell is that about?"

"Does anyone know where that voice came from?"

"Can anyone see any cameras or speakers of any kind?"

We start searching the room looking for cameras and speakers but there aren't any; the sound seemed to be coming straight through the walls. We all agree the voice sounded strange and what was said even stranger. At least 'he' said 'they' didn't want to hurt us, whoever 'they' are. He said when we meet them we can ask them questions, for me, that meeting can't come soon enough. The air in the room starts to feel different and we all start to feel really tired. We go back to our beds and as soon as we lie down we immediately fall asleep.

CHAPTER: TWO

"They will soon be radiation free."

"We will now leave them sedated until they are completely clear, then we will make arrangements to meet with them in person."

"The analytical device that we have secured around their necks is working as we wanted. The women are communicating freely with each other and we are receiving real time data on their physical and mental wellbeing back to our master data bank."

"Good. Do you know exactly when will they be radiation free?"

"Our calculations showed it would take three months for the radiation to disperse, which means the meeting will be able to take place in five days from now.

"Thank you, you may leave now."

....

I'm being shaken awake by Sal and she's shouting: *"Allie, wake-up, come and look, we can see outside."*

I open my eyes to what seems like natural light with Sal still urging me to come and look. As I sit up I can't believe what I'm seeing. What I thought was a wall has now been transformed into an enormous window. Again, this must have been done by unseen hands. It's really unnerving knowing someone has total control over our environment. First it was the lighting from nowhere - then the voice from nowhere - now a window from nowhere. What the hell will happen next? It feels like I've walked through the wardrobe and straight into Narnia!

There is enough room behind the beds and along the wall for all eighty of us to look out of the window. I can see what look like two different types of people moving around. To my left there is a very large aircraft of some description and it isn't like anything I've seen before. There are also three strange metallic structures that are similar in size to a garage or lock-up. The people in the vicinity of this aircraft appear to be a mix of males and females and they all appear to resemble each other in height and physique. Their clothing appears to be made of some sort of dark coloured material and on their feet they are wearing some kind of footwear made from the same material. The males are only wearing loose fitting trousers, showing a bare torso which looks all muscle. The others, I'm assuming females, have their torsos covered. They appear human as they have two arms, two legs, ears, eyes, nose and a mouth, but their whole appearance looks unkempt; they look almost tribal. It becomes obvious that the females are the dominant ones in this tribe, as they are issuing orders to the males who appear to be cowering whilst they obey.

The people, who are standing over to my right look completely different, more cultured looking. They all appear to be male; they are taller, slimmer and dressed uniformly in silvery grey jumpsuits and sturdy ankle length boots, giving them a military style appearance. They have congregated around a long block of these strange metallic looking buildings, but these ones are a lot bigger, almost like warehouses. Protruding from the rear of one of these warehouse type structures I can just make out something that looks like a truck of some sort. The ground directly in front of the window and stretching all the way to what I think is a terminal of some kind, is just a flat, smooth, featureless surface.

One of the military type men walks over to the nearest warehouse and raises his hand and a door magically slides open and out comes what I can only describe as a moving platform. It appears to be floating and stretches all the way from the warehouse until it disappears inside the aircraft. The rest of these men then take position either side of this platform and out of the aircraft comes what look like huge dark boulders or massive chunks of rock. It's now apparent that this platform is some kind of motorised conveyor belt, moving this rock from the aircraft directly into the warehouse. The men standing either side of the conveyor belt seem to be inspecting these chunks of rock as they pass. When there are no more rocks to be seen, the platform retracts right back into the warehouse and the door immediately slides shut.

The door to the next warehouse on the right opens and another moving platform starts to emerge. This platform is already loaded with what looks like large rust coloured hessian-type sacks, but this one stops when it reaches the rear of the aircraft. The females start to gesticulate to the males, who then begin to physically remove these sacks from the platform into the body of the aircraft. As soon as the last sack has been removed, the rest of the tribe disappear from view. Within seconds, I am amazed and alarmed as I watch this enormous machine, rapidly rise into a strange, cloudless yellow and amber sky and vanish into thin air. This platform immediately retracts back into the warehouse and the military looking men automatically clear the area of any debris. Whilst they are doing this, the truck I could see moves to the front of the building, then, in single file all the men climb aboard, again, giving the impression of a military unit.

·······

"Shall we phase out the window now?"

"No. Not yet."

"Why?"

"Leave it for a while, it will give the women more time to think about what they have seen and they should mention it at the meeting. They need to be aware of the Dreaki; they need to know how dangerous they could be to them. I do not think the Dreaki would be stupid enough to communicate with or try to take the women, but they are unpredictable so the women need to be warned."

....

The women have returned to their beds or are in groups talking amongst themselves. I'm still standing staring out of the window, even though there's nothing to see except silvery grey metal structures. I look up at the yellow and amber sky wondering where the hell I am. I've no idea what to make of what I've just seen, so I go and sit on Bea's bed as I want to know what she's thinking: *"Who do you think those people are and where do you think we could be?"*

"The ones who stayed definitely look and act like soldiers, it makes me wonder if we are being held in some kind of government facility, but God only knows which government! Did you notice the surroundings, apart from those buildings there was nothing else, it looks like we are in the middle of nowhere. Wherever we are, it is not looking good."

"The ones who left looked like they belonged to some sort of clan and that machine they took off in; I didn't think anything like that existed and what has happened to the sky, it's yellow and amber for God's sake?"

"It is not just the sky that's weird. Those others look in-bred to me and as soon as they had done what they had to do, that aircraft thing zoomed up into the sky like a bloody spaceship. All governments have secrets; they believe they are a law unto themselves."

"Why would any government be interested in eighty young women and bring us to a place that looks like some sort of terminal. As far as I could tell, they were trading with each other; it just looked like rocks for sacks."

"The voice said they are going to meet us, so hopefully when that happens, we might find out exactly where we are, why we are here and what the hell is going on."

I didn't know what else to say so I go back to my bed and just sit and stare at the window, which seemed to appear from nowhere, wondering what it's like out there and if I'll ever get to find out. I must be staring too hard as the window appears to be shrinking. Then I realise it's not me at all, the window is definitely shrinking and I'm not the only one looking at it. We are all transfixed, watching as the window becomes a wall again right in front of our eyes. The bastards, the one change that relieved this monotony they've taken away. As I'm lying here thoroughly pissed off, I can feel the change in the air, they are putting us to sleep again.

....

I'm woken up by the disembodied voice through the wall but at least the room is flooded with natural light – the window is back.

"Attention, Attention."

"You need to remove your clothing and go to the door in the wall opposite the window. When this door opens you are to go into the room. As you are no longer wearing healing sheaths it is necessary for your newly healed bodies to be given additional protection before encountering the external environment of this planet. When the door re-opens there will be more suitable clothing on your beds and it is compulsory that you wear this clothing whenever you are outside of this room. As soon as you have done this, the door at the end of the room will open and you are to get into the transport that will bring you to our Complex. All radiation has dispersed from your bodies and you are strong enough to meet us in person so we can now answer some of your questions."

As soon as the voice stops, we all remove our tunics and walk over to the wall, a control panel illuminates and the door slides open. I quickly step through the doorway; I'm so desperate to get out of this room. As I stand naked and shivering slightly, the rest of the women hesitantly join me until all of us are huddled together as the door slides shut. This room is slightly smaller than our room, with subdued lighting that gives everything a strange bluish cast. There are things on the ceiling that resemble shower heads. I look around at the expressions on the women's faces and can tell each one of us feels uneasy and frightened. The room reminds me of something I once saw in a long forgotten ancient history book and for a moment think, this could be it!

I can hear some of the women crying and others are rigid with fright. Then there is a 'buzzing' sound and then a 'whoosh'. It isn't really a shower as there isn't any water; it's more like a thick, cloudy vapour of some sort. I'm assuming this is their equivalent of a shower and this is how we keep ourselves clean and protect our bodies. I wish they could find a way to protect our minds as many of us are close to the edge.

Eventually the vapour in the room clears, all sound stops and the door re-opens. I quickly leave the room as instructed and can see some clothing has been placed on my bed. My new clothing resembles the jumpsuits worn by the men at the terminal. It feels extremely light and supple, solid footwear is incorporated into the legs; ultra thin gloves are incorporated into the sleeves and there is an ultra thin hood at the back. It's open at the front to allow me to climb in but as I begin to do this I nearly topple over. I sit on the bed and place my feet firmly into the attached footwear then pull the jumpsuit up my body until I can fit my arms into the sleeves and my hands into the gloves. I can't see an actual fastening but as soon as the sides come together the material seems to fasten seamlessly and the hood fits snugly around my head.

As soon as I've got myself into the jumpsuit I join the other women who are gathered around the door at the far end of the room and along the window. Out of the window I can see what look like Jeeps, lined up in a convoy. Another control panel illuminates and the door starts to slide open, there is a Jeep waiting outside the door. The doors of the Jeep are open and I can see there is a bench like seat at the front and one at the back. The women closest to the door get in, the doors close and the Jeep moves on allowing the second Jeep to do the same. I'm next in line; Bea, Jess and Sal get in with me. Our Jeep moves along to allow for the other Jeeps that are left.

I look up at the sky; it's the same strange mix of yellow and amber and there are still no clouds visible. I'm not experiencing any difficulty in breathing, I'm neither hot nor cold and I don't seem to be suffering any adverse affects at all. As the Jeep slowly moves along I look back at the building where I have been incarcerated, it looks longer than but not as high as the strange metallic looking buildings I saw from out of the window. All the Jeeps are being operated by some form of remote control, so this is something else we have no control over.

We then turn left away from the terminal and within a short distance the smooth surface that I can see from the window disappears. The Jeeps instantly accelerate as we travel on ground that is covered in uneven reddish-brown lumps that resemble clay, forcing us to hold onto the side as we bounce along. The uneven clay seems to go on forever and then the landscape becomes even more hostile. We are approaching an area where, as far as the eye can see, there are different sized hills made from the same reddish-brown clay. The Jeeps skilfully navigate these hills as they drive up and down and in-between with ease.

I seem to have lost all sense of direction but, as I turn my head to the left, I can just make out what looks like the top of the buildings at the terminal in the far distance. Suddenly, my view is completely obstructed as to my left the clay has risen up to form an embankment like ridge which seems to stretch for miles. Before reaching the end of this embankment all the Jeeps turn right, towards land that looks flatter and lighter in colour. The side of my face begins to feel warm, so I look up into the strange yellow and amber sky automatically seeking the sun. I have to shield my eyes as it's so bright and what I can see in the sky is nothing like the sun I was expecting to see. It appears to be in the shape of some sort of shell, not unlike the ones I used to collect as a child, only a zillion times bigger. The outside of the shell appears to be an even more powerful yellow than the sun I'm used to and being emitted from underneath this shell are amber coloured rays. Now I know why the sky looks so strange, the sun is even stranger!

When I next look forward I can see, in the distance, the outline of large metal buildings. As we approach, it's apparent these buildings are made of the same silvery grey metal as the buildings at the terminal, and the land we are now travelling on is the same flat smooth surface that we can see from our window. All of a sudden we stop, the doors of the Jeep at the head of the line open, four women get out, the Jeep moves on allowing the second Jeep to do the same. Our Jeep moves up, stops, Bea, Jess, Sal and I get out. We then wait for the other women to arrive from the remaining Jeeps. We have stopped in front of one of these buildings where there is a wide pathway that leads to two large entrance doors. It seems we have made an unspoken decision to move as one large group towards these doors, hoping there is strength in numbers. When we reach them, we just stand there as nobody knows what to do next. Do we knock on the door? Just go in? What?

This decision is made for us when both of these doors suddenly start to slide apart and a male looking figure appears. He is wearing the same silvery grey jumpsuit as the others we saw from the window, and before I can get a good look at him, he just says a single word *"follow"* then turns away from us and walks straight back into the building. We all bunch together, to try and stay as close to him as we can, as we follow him along a labyrinth of long corridors. There is sufficient lighting everywhere we turn but, as in our room, there are no light fittings or light switches anywhere to be seen. We eventually come to a halt at the end of one of these long corridors where we find ourselves facing a solid metal wall that has just one door in the centre. He raises his hand to the side of the door and some kind of computerised entry pad appears, as he places his hand over this pad the door immediately slides open. He stands to the side and ushers us into a large empty room; once we have all entered the door slides shut.

The first thing I notice is the room is flooded with natural light. Ahead of us is one enormous window which extends from one side of the wall to the other, from floor to ceiling. In front of this window there is a slightly raised area and at the far edge of this raised area on the right-hand side there appears to be a door, that's it, there's nothing else to be seen. We all gravitate towards the window and stop just before we reach the raised area, not knowing what will happen next. I turn to Sal and say: *"I'm going to take a closer look through that window and try and get a better look at what's out there."*

I'm just about to step onto the raised area when the door on the far right slides open. In file approximately forty to sixty people all wearing the same silvery grey jumpsuits. I watch as they all walk along the raised area in a military fashion until they are directly in front of us, then as one, they stop and just rigidly stand there in one long line. They all appear muscular, but differ slightly from each other in height, skin tone and hair colour, from where I'm standing they look no different to any other human being.

The last one through the door, however, is someone completely different; he's taller than the others with a slightly elongated and completely bald head. He appears human, like as in two arms, two legs but his facial features appear more sculptured than natural as does the rest of his body. Even his clothing doesn't seem quite natural almost like it's painted on. The skin on his hands, head and face looks strange as there appears to be a slight metallic sheen to them. He walks to the centre of the line and stands with the others. There are a lot of people in this room and not a sound can be heard. The one who looks different, steps forward, raises his hand, then

CTJ Reeves: Asmeron

speaks: *"I realise you will have many questions and I will endeavour to answer as many as I can. Some I may not be able to answer at this time. So, firstly, I will explain where you are and who we are:*

This is the same strange, monotone voice that had frightened us all half to death earlier.

Due to the nuclear devastation of Earth we have brought you to a completely different solar system. This planet you are now on, we have called Asmeron. We arrived here four years ago but these are not Earth years. There are only two planets left in this solar system, this one and a neighbouring planet called Dreakoria. All of the other planets have either been obliterated due to natural disasters, by different species destroying each other, or, as with your own planet, the same species destroying themselves. This is not our native planet and we are neither humans nor aliens. We were designed and created by humans from your planet Earth. A group of eminent scientists created a colony within your solar system, on the planet called Ceres, with the intention of manufacturing the right atmospheric conditions to mimic Earth. This planet could then be used to accommodate some of the ever increasing population that was depleting the natural resources of their home planet.

The first thing that was needed was a workforce, a workforce that required neither food nor rest. To this aim the Researchers' designed and created androids, of which I am one. I am a synthetic organism built with complex algorithms giving me the ability to learn. The others you see here are humanoids, designed and created like me, but they have a biological base which means that they can not only learn but also evolve. The Researchers' dream was that over time and with interaction with humans they would become human themselves. During their time on Ceres the Researchers became disillusioned with the human race and were convinced that the egotistical leaders on your planet would eventually annihilate everyone and your planet would have to start again.

This is why they were determined to create a new life form; a life form that would continue to evolve but be as non-violent as possible. With the superior learning capability of the androids, their research advanced phenomenally but it still took many years and many failures before the final breakthrough. A completely new biological life form was created using the Researchers' own DNA. Some of these life forms are the humanoids you see before you. The Researchers, however, were only human and as such subject to the realities of time and illness. We androids, being technologically advanced, were able to prolong their lives by some years but, unfortunately, they succumbed one by one until there was only one Researcher left, Professor Crawford. He was one hundred and fifteen years old, but he did not die of old age. Ceres was becoming unstable, so we constructed an interstellar spacecraft to evacuate the newly developed humanoids to ensure their survival. The androids most involved with the creation of the humanoids were chosen to continue to uphold their evolution and keep the Researchers' dream alive. The Professor decided to remain on Ceres with the remaining androids hoping to construct a second interstellar spacecraft in time for their escape. Unfortunately time was against them, as shortly after we left Ceres the whole planet imploded leaving nothing and no-one behind.

What has since occurred, that was not envisaged, is the humanoids evolving at a speed far greater than the Researchers could ever have imagined. This, in turn, led to our survival and eventually we found this planet we call Asmeron. I am sure you have many questions, I will now try and answer as many as I am able to."

A woman whose name is Simone, is first to put up her hand: "You said you have been living on Asmeron for four years but these are not Earth years. What do you mean?"

"This planet, Asmeron, takes far longer to rotate than Earth. This gives us far longer days but also longer and colder nights. Asmeron also takes longer to rotate around its sun, this means that the years, as you know them, are also far longer."

Another woman raises her hand: *"How long have we been here?"*

"You have been on Asmeron for three of our months, for most of that time you have been sedated in order for your bodies to heal. You are all now radiation free and your bodies are becoming stronger with each day."

Another hand shoots up, it's Dr Chi: *"Whilst I appreciate the fact that you have rescued and healed us, I have to ask why and why so few of us?"*

"We were aware of the conflict that had overtaken your planet and knew it would only be a matter of time before the Researchers worst fears were realised and the leaders of your planet chose to wilfully destroy each other without thought for the consequences. Each leader thinking their nation was the most superior and would be the only ones to survive. Using an interstellar spacecraft, similar to the one we had escaped Ceres in; we came to Earth but we were too late to stop the final devastation. With the time that was allowed us and the capacity of our

spacecraft, at that time, we were restricted on who could be saved."

Another hand immediately shoots in the air followed by the rapid questions: *"Why have you only saved women? Why are there no men or children here?"*

"As I have stated previously, we were restricted by both time and capacity."

I think to myself, I don't think that's the whole truth, it just doesn't make sense.

The next question comes from Bea: *"Will we be allowed to leave the room that we have been incarcerated in and move around more freely?"*

"We have given this some thought and we feel you are now strong enough to leave your room for the purpose of physical exercise and mental stimulation. Before you leave the room you must always use the vapour unit each morning, in order to continue to cleanse and protect your bodies and, until your bodies adjust to the environment here, you must always wear the outdoor clothing you are wearing now. It is imperative that you return to your room as soon as the light starts to fade."

Bea then jumps back in with: *"Why can't we stay out after the light starts to fade?"*

"When the sun fades from Asmeron's sky it becomes extremely dark, extremely quickly and the temperature drops well below the tolerance level of your human bodies."

One of the younger ones, Mattie, nervously says: *"Will we be able to use the Jeeps?"*

"Yes. The Jeeps were to be used by the workforce on Ceres and they have been adapted for your use. There are seven commands, forward, left, right, faster, slower, reverse and stop."

Sal asks: *"Does it rain here?"*

"No, there is no precipitation of any kind on this planet. There are, however, vast quantities of water forming many underground streams. We believe these originate from the frozen wasteland on this planet. This is not water as you know from Earth, it is extremely acidic and would be corrosive to your human skin. Some of these streams lie very close to the surface which makes the land there extremely fertile. We have installed vast water butts underneath a place we call the Plantation. These are interconnected with channels similar to what you may know as irrigation channels."

Before anyone else can stick up their hand, mine goes up: *"Who were the other people we could see from the window and why do they come here?"*

"They are from the neighbouring planet they call Dreakoria. The Dreaki come to Asmeron every twenty-one days in order to trade. The Plantation is where a certain type of food is grown, this has been designed and cultivated in order for us to trade with the Dreaki for the resources we need. The Dreaki have overpopulated their planet and are now lacking the fertile land and resources to feed themselves and are reliant on the food we supply to ensure the survival of their species."

I take this opportunity to ask the question that I've been waiting to ask: *"Talking about food, we have neither eaten nor drank any fluid since we have been here, and yet we are suffering from no adverse affects, how is this possible?"*

"We know exactly what your bodies need in both nourishment and fluid in order to survive. Unfortunately the plant life and the water on this plant cannot be tolerated by your human digestive system at this time. You will have realised that you all have two implants underneath the skin on your left arm; one implant has been designed to provide all the nutrition that your bodies need. The second implant keeps your bodily tissue at the

right level of hydration. These implants ensure there are no toxins dispersed into your bodies and will last approximately nine months."

Irina puts her hand up next: *"You keep saying years and months but tell us these are different to the ones on Earth, so how do you know how long nine months is?"*

"Asmeron's moon has similar phases to the moon on Earth so we use these phases to calculate time going from one full moon to the next, what you would know as a lunar month, so every nine full moons your implants will need to be changed."

Jess's hand is up next: *"If the collar around our neck enables us to communicate with each other, will it enable us to communicate with the Dreaki?"*

"No. Under no circumstances are you to interact with the Dreaki. They are an untrustworthy and extremely aggressive species. The female is both dominant and treacherous and whilst the male may be subservient he is also cunning. Whilst they are no threat to us, as they cannot harm us, they would be extremely dangerous to you."

Jess immediately asks: *"Why? What will they do to us?"*

"Rip you to pieces."

None of us like that answer. Some of the women are visibly upset. I glance at Bea and know it isn't just me who isn't sure about the agenda of these 'people'. I'm starting to feel very uneasy about what is being said. I'm not sure the android is being honest with us. Why have they incarcerated us so close to the Dreaki if they are that dangerous. Jess must be thinking the same thing as she looks uneasy and Sal is visibly upset. Judging by the expression on Bea's face she's as suspicious as I am. I think I'll talk to her, on her own, later.

One of the younger ones; Sameena, interrupts my train of thought by asking: *"Can we explore wherever we want, like where you grow the food as that must be less barren than here?"*

"No. It is not possible for you to reach the Plantation and return to your room before the light fades. Many of your explorations will be limited due to time. When we first arrived here we constructed aircrafts to allow us to thoroughly explore Asmeron. Our explorations showed this planet has three distinct zones. The first zone is a frozen wasteland and when we attempted to make an assessment of this area a number of our humanoids and androids were damaged beyond repair. The polar opposite to this frozen wasteland is an area covered in shifting sand. This exploration also resulted in disaster as we underestimated the rapidity of this shifting sand

and the remaining androids and several humanoids disappeared without trace. These areas can therefore only be observed from the air. The third and largest zone is the one we are in now and according to our assessments is safe. This Complex is also not accessible to you, unless you are summoned."

I can tell he is getting ready to dismiss us when Bea says: "Are you the only one that can speak? If these humanoids are so advanced, why is it that you are the only one communicating with us?"

Before he can respond the humanoid standing to the side of the android, takes a step forward and responds to Bea's question: **"All humanoids can and will communicate verbally. We also have the ability to communicate non-verbally with each other using our collective consciousness. Eventually we will be communicating with you on an individual basis."**

The android abruptly says: **"The light will be fading soon and you must all now be returned to your room. We will speak again shortly."**

With that he turns and begins to leave the room followed immediately by the humanoid who had spoken. The other humanoids turn as one to follow them out. The last in the line approaches us and leads us back out of the building to our waiting transport.

When we get back into the Jeep, I make sure I'm sat next to Bea. *"What do you think? Did you believe him?"* I whisper.

"No not all of it. Too many things didn't add up, especially that bit about being unable to save any men or children."

"What about what he said about those others, what did he call them, Dreaki?"

"They look feral and the females seem aggressive, so he could be telling the truth about them."

Sal's starting to cry, she just manages to say: *"What do you think Allie? Is everyone really dead, my whole family just gone?"*

"It seems that way Sal. I'm struggling to believe it myself. If they are telling the truth and we are the only ones left; then we have to stick together. We are all in shock and we are all scared. It's going to take time to accept what's happened to everybody on earth, to loved ones, to us. We may have to accept that the life we knew is now over, everything has now changed."

The Jeeps start to move and we begin our journey back to the room. I'm sure a lot of the women, like me, will feel that this meeting has raised more questions than it has answered.

CHAPTER: THREE

"I have called this meeting as I need to speak to all of you. The meeting with the women did not go as I had anticipated. It is obvious some of them did not like some of the things that were said. I do not want these women to know about any of the Researchers future plans. It is far too early to tell them that there is to be interaction between them and yourselves. They need more time to familiarise themselves with and adjust to being on Asmeron and it will take time to gain their trust. Giving them some freedom may be one way to alleviate this problem.

I also need time to examine all the data in detail before I can make any decisions regarding interaction. Due to the circumstances of the woman called, Bea, I am the obvious choice, but I need to decide which of the women will be more responsive and which of you will be chosen first for this interaction."

"I cannot agree to this."

"Why?"

CTJ Reeves: Asmeron

"If there is to be interaction between ourselves and the women then it is up to us to choose who we will interact with. I have chosen to try and interact with the woman called, Allie."

"I do not understand why you have singled out this particular woman, explain."

"I do not fully understand why, I just know this is what I have chosen. The women should also be able to choose which of us they want to interact with."

"I do not agree with you on this and as we need an answer to this dilemma immediately we will take a count of everyone's opinion. Those of you who agree with me stand with me, those of you who disagree with me, are to stand with you....this is the first time any of you have opposed me and I find this situation very disconcerting but as the majority is in favour of you deciding for yourselves, I reluctantly accept this decision."

"We will need time to study the data in greater detail and suggest any interaction takes place once this has been done."

"As you have stated it is no longer my decision to make. You can all return to your duties now."

This is the first time they have all gone against me like this. I have got to try and understand their thinking. It is for the good of us all that the right decisions are made regarding these women. I understand now some of the conversations that had taken place when the humanoids were first created. The Researchers were right....as now it begins!

CHAPTER: FOUR

As soon as I'm back in the dormitory the jumpsuit loosens and is no longer fixed in place. I sit on my bed and climb out of the jumpsuit and put my tunic back on as it feels less restrictive. I've no sooner done this when the women start shouting out questions:

Jess is first: *"What do they mean they will be communicating with us on an individual basis?"*

Bea answers this one: *"What do you think it means. There is obviously a reason why they brought us here, maybe they will tell us and maybe they won't. If we start talking to them and asking questions we can pool any information we find out."*

A woman called Tori shouts: *"What if we don't want to communicate with 'them'. 'It' said they were created by humans so they are not human. How do you talk to a bloody machine?"*

This time I jump in: *"To be honest, we don't really know what they are, what they know, what they are capable of and more importantly, what they want from us. Whether we like it or not, it's obvious they are more intelligent than we are. Also, whether they are men or machines, they can hurt us far more than we can hurt them. Bea is right, the situation we are in it makes sense to communicate with them. What is it people used to say about hostage situations, make your captors think of you as an individual and there is less likelihood they will hurt you."*

Another woman, Maria, looks at me and spits out: *"So is that what we are, hostages? They had no right bringing us here. Someone needs to demand they tell us why they brought us here and what they plan to do with us."*

"Maria, there is absolutely nothing at all any of us can do about this. I know as much as you, that's why we need to communicate with them. What would you suggest? For God's sake, we don't actually have the upper hand here. We are on a planet in a completely different solar system for a start. We need to know what they are up to; we need to know if they are telling us the truth. I find it hard to believe that out of nine billion people we are the only eighty to survive and what are the odds on the only survivors all being female. There are so many things we need to know and talking to them may be the only way of finding out the truth."

Sal joins in: *"How do we go about talking to them? Do we go up to them, will they approach us? To be honest Allie, they scare me."*

"I think all of us feel scared. We're in a bizarre situation. According to them we've been here for over three months, whatever that means here. The android said they didn't want to hurt us, also after what happened on Earth our bodies would have been severely damaged, yet they've healed us. Until we can find out more about them, we'll just have to take each day as it comes and see what happens."

Bea then addresses us all: *"Taking each day as it comes is all we can do. I suggest we wait and see if they approach us. I, like Allie, want answers to questions but I think we need to have our wits about us. We need to get as much information out of them as possible without them realising what we are doing."*

Everyone starts to calm down and return to their beds. We all know there is absolutely nothing any of us can do to change our situation. I'm just hoping the air will get heavy as I think we all might need some help to sleep.

CHAPTER: FIVE

Morning is here and I'm buzzing. I can't wait to see what's out there. The control panel to the vapour unit has become luminous and as soon as someone puts their hand over it, the door slides open. We all get into the vapour unit together and as soon as the procedure has finished we put on our jumpsuits and make our way to the door at the far end of the room. As soon as the control panel illuminates, the woman at the front of the line places her hand over the control panel and the door slides open. I'm so excited; no longer being stuck in a room with a load of other women is going to be absolute bliss.

As soon as we are outside the room, everyone makes their way to one of the Jeeps that are parked in a convoy outside the door; there are twenty of them so we know we have to share. Bea, Jess, Sal and I get into a Jeep and wait for the ones in front of us to move on. We've been told they are voice activated and we have to use one of seven commands forward, left, right, faster, slower, reverse and stop. Initially, we all drive slowly as one by one everyone turns left away from the terminal. When we are no longer driving on the flat smooth surface, the four of us decide to take turns giving the

Jeep instructions. I go first, I increase the speed only a little, but I still struggle to navigate the uneven reddish-brown clay. Sal goes next; she's slightly better than me, then Jess takes over, speeds up and doesn't appear to find navigating a challenge. Bea is now eager to have a go, she tells the Jeep to drive at full speed; she's a natural and takes to it like a duck to water.

It feels like we've been driving around for hours and we still haven't seen anything I consider remotely interesting. All I can see is never ending lumps of reddish brown clay and I'm already sick of the sight of it. Bea and Jess have taken over navigating, they have taken us to the region where there are mounds of this clay that look like hills and are having great fun driving up and down and weaving in and out of these hills. The Jeeps are slower than when they were remote controlled, but they still go fast enough for us to bounce up and down. Sal and I are starting to feel nauseous and have had enough, so we ask Bea and Jess to take us back. Reluctantly they agree and after making a few wrong turns they eventually navigate our way back to what we now think of as the dormitory.

CHAPTER: SIX

If there's a Jeep free I go out with Sal, hoping we can find somewhere, anywhere, that isn't covered in reddish-brown clay. Some of the women actually enjoy driving on this stuff and often go to the areas where the mounds of clay look like hills. Bea and Jess are part of this clique that takes part in what they call off-road racing; they've even turned it into a competitive sport. The rules of the game are; they choose different circuits, where they will start and where they will finish, then two Jeeps at a time, with two women in each Jeep, race against each other navigating the uneven clay, driving up and down and in and out of the hills. The winners then take on the next two women waiting in line and off they go again.

I've had enough of driving around on this bloody clay, day-in, day-out, so I've been asking around to see if any of the women are interested in getting some activities going, as we need to find other things to do in order to break the monotony of everyday living. I'm pleasantly surprised to find a lot of the women feel the same way as me, so we are putting our heads together to try and come up with some ideas that will keep the majority of us occupied. Now more and more of us are starting to stay in the room again, it's not long before petty squabbles begin. Most of us get on well, but not all of us.

Three of the women, Maria, Christa and Grace are wind-up merchants and can be spiteful at times. Also, with so many women being forced to live together, there's bound to be personality clashes so, every now and then, they let rip and sparks fly. Some of the women are just miserable buggers and continually moan and groan and a few of the women still keep taking to their beds as they seem unable to cope in general. A woman called Tori is the biggest troublemaker amongst us; she's loud, obnoxious; and a bully. She tries to intimidate and belittle the younger women or anyone with little confidence and low self-esteem. She's quite tall and well-built, not overweight, more muscle than fat, similar to Bea. Unlike Bea, she has an air of menace about her and I know a lot of the women are scared of her. She's been trying to scupper some of the activities I want to get started, but as more women become interested in what I want to do, she's had to back off. Now she just avoids me as much as possible, which suits me just fine.

We have finally agreed on a number of things we are going to do. We are going to play old fashioned parlour games, such as charades, even children's games, although I'm guessing eye-spy is out! We are all still trying to think of games that were played before technology took over. We are also going to start four types of exercise classes Pilates, Aerobics, Yoga, and for the women who want to do something more physical, we are going to start a Boxercise class, but no bullies will be allowed.

We are all looking forward to improving our well-being by taking part in the Yoga classes and increasing our endorphins by taking part in physical exercise. Luckily all the beds are ultra-light so, before each class begins, we will be able to upend the beds and line them along the walls leaving us plenty of room, which means will be able to hold more than one class at a time.

CHAPTER: SEVEN

Bea, Jess and Sal have decided I've been spending too much time in the dormitory and have persuaded me to go for a drive round. I suppose it will be good to have a change of scene and it will be nice just the four of us spending some time together. They have promised not go to the hilly area and, as we leave the terminal, instead of turning left Bea points the Jeep straight ahead and we drive directly away from the dormitory. After we've been driving around for a while I start to feel disheartened again as everywhere still looks the same. Just as we are about to turn back and head 'home', we hit a large lump of clay. This causes us to veer to the left and the Jeep suddenly comes to a stop, we get out and check if there's any visible damage, we can't see any.

As we look around we notice there is an area where the ground appears to be different, we can see ahead of us what looks like a gravel pathway. The further we walk along this pathway we find there are different sized rocks everywhere and strewn between these rocks there are lots of different sized stones. As we explore, we come across another pathway that is in-between two very large rocks. This pathway leads us to an area that looks like some sort of monument as everything appears to have been strategically placed in an almost perfect semi-circle. I immediately think of Stonehenge, as huge rock formations appear to have taken the shape of large pillars and they all appear to be of an equal distance from each other.

As we continue to walk around this monument like structure, I'm convinced it was put here deliberately and could have been here for hundreds, thousands or millions of years, a lot longer than the four years the android and humanoids have been here anyway. In-between these pillars there are millions of small stones and surrounding the area there are similar sized rocks and each one has a flat surface. We help each other climb onto one of these rocks where the flat surface is big enough for all four of us to sit together. Jess says: *"It looks like something might have once existed here; these rocks could be all that's left of some sort of past civilisation? What do you three think?"*

Bea goes first: *"You could be right; I can see no reason why the humanoids would have built something like this. They say they have only been on this planet for four years and these rocks could have been here for thousands and thousands of years, if not more. To me, it looks like some sort of ancient monument. Maybe there was a species here before the androids and humanoids arrived and this place was special to* them in some way, maybe they held sacrifices here. Allie, what do you think?"

"I don't know if they held sacrifices, but it does looks like a monument of some sort. I'm no expert, but these rocks could have been here for hundreds, thousands or even millions of years. It reminds me of something in my own country and for all we know there could have been something like this on every planet in the Universe, until natural forces or an unhinged species, including our own, obliterated everything."

The three of us look at Sal, waiting for her to say something: *"I have no idea why it is here, does it even matter. If you are right, then it seems there is nowhere in the universe that is of any use, to anyone, anymore. I am going to ask Mattie and Sameena to come here with me. We could have fun trying to climb some of the rocks."*

With that we decide to leave. We slowly make our way back to the Jeep and are all relieved when it automatically starts.

CHAPTER: EIGHT

The monotony of trying to occupy myself during the long days has been a nightmare, now I have more things to do to the days pass far easier. I still go out in a Jeep now and then, in the hope of finding somewhere different. Sal often goes off with Mattie and Sameena to the area I call the stones and Bea and Jess spend a lot of their time off-road racing with Irina and Simone. I've always been interested in mental health and physical exercise, so I lead a Yoga class and a Boxercise class and, in the absence of any equipment, I concentrate on shadow boxing, footwork, squats, star jumps and light sparing. Bea, Jess and Sal often take part in my Boxercise class and occasionally they will join in with the silly, but fun, games we play.

Today, I need a break from the troublemakers, the moaners and those who seem constantly depressed. Sal has already gone out, so I've asked Bea and Jess if they will come with me to the stones. They agree, providing I navigate and I travel at a faster speed and not at a snail's pace. My navigating skills are definitely improving and as we arrive at the stones, we see three other Jeeps are already here. We are just about to take the pathway that leads to the monument when Sal, Mattie and

Sameena appear from nowhere. Bea and Jess say 'hi'; then carry on walking. I stay and talk to them for a while, then watch as they sprint off in high spirits, then I carry on walking towards the monument to catch up with Bea and Jess.

As I get nearer to the monument I can see Bea, Irina, Jess and Simone standing by one of the pillars, Bea is talking to Maria and Grace. I'm surprised to see these two without their friend Christa as they are always together, like the three stooges. I don't particularly want to join them, so I sit on one of the rocks close by, close enough to hear what they are saying. I can hear Maria and Grace asking Bea about the monument. Bea's telling them she thinks the monument could have been built by an old civilisation. She's explaining she thinks this place could have been somewhere they considered special, maybe they held meetings here, or, it could have been a place where sacrifices were made. Maria and Grace seem to be fascinated with what Bea is saying and are hanging on to her every word.

As soon as Maria and Grace leave, I join the others. I've enjoyed spending a bit of time on my own and I'm enjoying the company of Bea, Irina, Jess and Simone. The hours seem to fly by and it's now time for us to leave. On our way back to the Jeep we call out to Sal, Mattie and Sameena; just in case they have lost all sense of time. We hear them before we see them, as they are laughing and clowning around. We all jump into the Jeeps we came in and head back to the dormitory.

As we enter the room everyone goes quiet and I immediately pick up on an unpleasant atmosphere, I'm guessing the women have been arguing yet again. Sal and I walk over to our beds, which are now next to each other; we've only just sat down, when it all kicks off. Maria, Christa and Grace are ranting and raving. Grace is screaming: *"None of you know what these things are planning to do with us. We should be demanding they tell us why they brought us here and what for? I've seen that place where they sacrifice people. These things that have control of us are not human. I hate it here; I don't want to be on this God forsaken planet!"*

Maria and Christa join in: *"Grace is right; these things that are keeping us here are nothing more than machines, at least the others that come here, might look primitive, but at least they look human. We didn't ask to come here, we don't want to be here and they have no right keeping us here!"*

On and on they go. They remind me of a play written by Shakespeare that my grandmother once told me about, so, I'm nicknaming the three of them: Hubble, Bubble, Toil and Trouble, with Grace being Toil and Trouble. It doesn't take long before some of the other women start to join in. Some of them agree with Maria, Christa and Grace whilst others think we should just be grateful to still be alive.

I knew it would only be a matter of time, before the pent-up frustration the women feel was let loose. Tempers are now getting out of control and the situation is becoming violent. First, the pushing and slapping starts, then hard punches are being thrown. The women who fall to the floor are being kicked en-mass. As soon as this happens the 'three witches' quickly move well away from it all, but Tori and her buddies, Florence, Nina and Andrea get stuck in. It's starting to become all-out-war, as about thirty of the women are now screaming at each other and rolling around on the floor. I'm wondering whether to get involved when I see Bea walk towards them. I'm sure she's going to join in the fight when she stops and bellows: *"All of you stop fighting and shut the fuck up!"* and to everyone's surprise, they do!

CHAPTER: NINE

"I have asked you to come here to talk about what happened in the room. This proves the women are not ready for any individual interaction by us. I know you and the other humanoids communicate with each other regularly using your collective consciousness, so I want to know what has been said and why you think the women reacted the way they did."

"We believe it is time to move them out of the room and bring them into the Complex."

"Why?"

"Just giving them more freedom has not achieved what we thought it would. We do not think the Researchers would have considered it natural for so many humans to be in one room for as long as they have been. As we have seen, this has resulted in an explosive situation."

"Why do you think moving them amongst us is a good idea?"

"Leaving them where they are is no longer viable. They need to be given their own accommodation and to be

separated from each other as much as possible. We can reconstruct one of the buildings into forty separate rooms and each room will contain two beds. We will need to incorporate more vapour units and we think they will need a large open room should they wish to congregate with each other. We have also observed that some of the women are spending too much time watching the Dreaki when they come to trade and we have equally noticed that the male Dreaki are spending too much time watching them."

"I think by letting them live amongst us, they will become more hostile towards us and that will have a negative effect on our future plans."

"The majority of us disagree and it is a majority decision that the women can no longer remain in one room. Also by bringing them into the Complex they will get used to seeing us on a daily basis and this may decrease any hostility towards us. We have already decided on which building is to be remodelled."

"As this decision has already been made, there is nothing more to be said."

CHAPTER: TEN

I have no sympathy whatsoever for those women who now have black eyes and are covered in bruises. Now they have got rid of some of their frustration they appear to be a lot more subdued but with so many of them no longer talking to each other the atmosphere in the room is dire. To make matters worse the Dreaki are trading today, so I am stuck in this bloody room for the next few hours, but as soon as the Dreaki and humanoids have left the terminal, I'm out of here.

At last, trading is over and the terminal is empty. I've grabbed a Jeep and, for some unearthly reason, I'm heading for the hills. I'm going to try and get rid of some of my own frustration by copying Bea and Jess; I'm going to have a go at off-road racing. After, what feels like, hours of driving up and down and in and out of these bloody hills, I've had enough. Bea and Jess always feel invigorated when they've been off-road racing; I just ache all over and feel exhausted.

As soon as I get back to the dormitory I lie down on my bed. I must have immediately fallen asleep because when I next open my eyes the light outside has completely faded. There is still enough light emitting from the control panels for me to see

Bea; she's walking around the room. She's realised I'm awake and is now walking towards my bed, as soon as she's near enough I whisper: *"Why are you walking around? Is something wrong?"*

"'Yes. Maria, Christa and Grace are missing."

"What! Are you sure? How can they be missing; there's nowhere to go missing to!"

"They are not in their beds and I have looked everywhere, which took all of ten seconds. They are not in this room."

"Can you remember when you last saw them?"

"They were definitely in the room when the Dreaki first arrived. What about you?"

"To be honest, since they've stopped moaning I haven't taken much notice of them. Do you think their Jeep might have broken down or they've had an accident?"

"No, I don't think that. I have been watching them for some time. I think they have been planning something for a while. They are always the first ones at the window when the Dreaki come to trade. They just stand there the whole time, staring at a group of the male Dreaki and, more than once, I have noticed that same group staring back at them. I hate to say this Allie, but I think they have either gone with or been taken by the Dreaki."

"That's not possible; someone would have seen them."

"Not necessarily, those three buildings near to where the Dreaki craft lands, could have given them enough cover, especially if the Dreaki were encouraging them in some way. The humanoids are always focused on doing whatever it is they do. I think they could have easily got too close to the Dreaki without anyone seeing them. This is when they could have snatched them; unless they went with them by choice."

"Christ Bea, if you're right, this is bad. The android and humanoids always seem to know what we're doing, before we do. Do you think they already know what's happened to them?"

"If they do, they are not sharing any information with us. We can't go out until it gets light because of the temperature but, as soon as it is, we will let the rest of the women know and then we will all have to try and find our own way to that place where we had the meeting. Maybe then we will find out if they already know or not. Is that ok with you?"

"Yes, I can't see what else we can do."

"Allie, if the Dreaki are as dangerous as we have been told, then these women are in serious, serious trouble. I do not expect we'll get much sleep but we will talk again as soon as it is light."

Bea goes back to her bed and I try to go back to sleep. I can't believe these women would have gone voluntary with the Dreaki. Surely, they wouldn't be that stupid! Perhaps curiosity got the better of them and they just got too close.

I've been tossing and turning for most of the night, so I haven't had much sleep. As I sit up I can see Bea is already talking to the women. I walk over to where everyone has congregated and can hear Bea explain what she thinks may have happened. I can't believe the attitude of some of the women; it can only be described as heartless. They either don't give a shit, or think, Maria, Christa and Grace deserve everything they get. Thankfully, there are enough of us who still have enough compassion left and who are willing to search for them, but no-one wants to get involved enough to meet with the android. They've asked if Bea and I will go. I would prefer us to go en-mass; as the android made it clear that the Complex was off limits. The women won't budge, so, Bea and I reluctantly agree to go on our own.

As soon as we leave the terminal we turn left, and head towards the Complex, both of us visualising the journey ahead. I'm so pleased Bea's with me as she's driving at full speed and has no problem navigating the uneven clay. I must have caught up on some sleep before we reached the hilly region, as I don't remember Bea navigating our way through it, and I can see on our left, where the clay has risen up to form an embankment like ridge which appears to go on forever. We travel alongside the embankment until we recognise where we have to turn right, we can see the land becoming flatter and lighter in colour. We carry on in this direction for a long time until we see the outline of the buildings we are looking for. We turn into the Complex and start driving on the smooth surface that is at the terminal and can now see the building where we had the meeting. We stop the Jeep, get out and approach the two imposing metal doors and then we both stop at the same time.

"Allie, are you OK?"

"Yes, but I'm really nervous about being here."

"I am as well but we need their help, are you ready?"

"Yes."

We are just about to bang on the metal doors when they start to slide apart and a humanoid appears: **"You are not allowed here. What do you want?**

Bea stands her ground and firmly says: "We need to speak to the android, it's an emergency. We need to speak to him now!"

The humanoid just says: **"Wait here."**

Then he goes back into the building and leaves the two doors open. We are tempted to follow him into the building but as we know we're not allowed here, we have no idea as to what the android's reaction will be. After what feels like forever but was probably just a few minutes, the humanoid reappears: **"Follow me."**

We follow him down a labyrinth of corridors, none of which we recognise. Soon we are outside another metal door. The humanoid actually knocks on the door and waits until it slides open. As we walk into the room, the android just stands there, staring at us: **"You say there is an emergency and you need to speak to me, why?"**

Both of us hesitate and then Bea starts to explain: *"Three of our women are missing; we think they have been taken by the Dreaki. I'm sure you are aware there was a fight in our room recently. These women cannot adapt to being on Asmeron. When the Dreaki come to trade they are the first ones at the window and the last ones to leave. Recently I have noticed a small group of the male Dreaki focusing on these women and the women focusing on them, it's as though they are trying to make contact with each other. Since the fight, the behaviour of these women changed. They are usually argumentative but they have been unusually quiet and staying out of everyone's way. We were so pleased they had stopped making trouble;*

we just took no notice of them, that's why none of us noticed them leaving the room. Do you know where they are?"

After a few minutes the android responds: **"We are aware that these women are no longer on Asmeron, they are on Dreakoria. What we do not understand is why they put themselves in a position where this could happen. What is it you want me to do?"**

"Arrange for some humanoids to go to Dreakoria and bring the women back."

"I cannot do this. You were all warned to stay away from the Dreaki. These women chose to ignore that warning. We are non-violent and if the Dreaki do not want to return these women to Asmeron there is nothing we can do. The Dreaki, on the other hand, are a depraved species which means these women will no longer be the same women as those who left here. There is nothing I can do and there is nothing more to be said."

As soon as the android finishes speaking, the humanoid steps into the room and escorts us back to our Jeep. Neither Bea nor I can believe that's it. He's not going to help in any way; the bastard is just going to leave Maria, Christa and Grace with those creatures. Bea and I are both initially speechless and feel helpless as there's absolutely nothing we can do. We quietly and solemnly begin our long journey back to the dormitory. I'm still trying to make sense of the android's sheer indifference when Bea says: "The android's obviously in charge and he has no intention of helping them."

"I can't believe they're just going to leave them on Dreakoria. God knows what those things are doing to them. If we mean so little to them, why did they bother rescuing us in the first place?

"I don't know?"

"How do you think the women will react?"

"We will find out soon enough."

We've now reached the hilly region and Bea is concentrating, navigating our way through. Soon we'll be back in the dormitory and I'm dreading having to face the women.

The light is starting to fade and as soon as we enter the room. Everyone gathers round us waiting for one of us to speak. Jess gets impatient and says: "Did you speak to the android? Does he already know Maria, Christa and Grace are missing?

"Yes."

Sal asks: "Does he know if they have been taken by the Dreaki?"

"He confirmed the women are on Dreakoria and that no-one will be bringing them back to Asmeron."

"What! He's just going to leave them there! The bastard! Why won't he make the Dreaki bring them back?"

I let Bea answer this one: *"As far as he is concerned the women have brought this upon themselves. He also implied they are already beyond help. He refused to say anything more to us. A humanoid turned up and ushered Allie and I out of the building."*

A friend of Tori's, Nina speaks next: *"Some of us agree with the android and think it's their own fault."*

Dr Jenna responds: *"Thankfully those of you who feel this way are in the minority.*

Simone jumps in with: *"Allie is that it; the women are going to be left on Dreakoria forever?"*

"It looks that way."

I don't feel like answering any more questions, but I can see Irina wants to ask something. As I walk away I hear her ask her question and Bea answer: *"What if something happens to one of us; will they just leave us to rot?"*

"None of us know the answer to that one."

I carry on walking over to the window and just stare into the darkness, wondering what the hell is happening to Maria, Christa and Grace!

CHAPTER: ELEVEN

"They did not react well to what you said to them."

"They were all warned to stay away from the Dreaki. We were complacent in monitoring these three women. It is in our interest to leave them on Dreakoria."

"There are a large number of us who do not think this way. If we just leave these women at the hands of the Dreaki we believe it will have a detrimental effect on the rest of the women."

"This situation is not worth becoming hostile with the Dreaki. We all need to remember our aim is to be non-violent and our coding is to defend ourselves only."

"We do not need to use violence. We will communicate with them and ask them to return the women; if they refuse, it will be made clear their food supply will be reduced."

"I do not agree with this but if it is a majority decision it will be done. The penalty the women will pay for their lunacy is high as they will never function properly again. There needs to be a vote."

CHAPTER: TWELVE

The despised Dreaki should be here soon to trade. I can't believe it's been twenty-one days since the women were taken. Since we have been allowed outside this room the control panel on the door has always remained illuminated, so we can come and go as we please. Today it's been deactivated; we are locked-in. Unexpectedly, the intercom comes back to life, causing us all to jump in surprise.

"Attention. The three women are being returned today."

I can't believe what I'm hearing. My feelings are all over the place. They never told us if the women were dead or alive. We are all standing along the wall looking out of the window. I'm starting to think they aren't coming. Suddenly the Dreaki craft appears from nowhere and as soon as they appear from the rear of the craft, trading begins.

The first platform, laden with rocks, has just retracted into the warehouse. The platform laden with the brown sacks appears, but this time something is different. A large quantity of the hessian sacks are being taken off the platform by the humanoids and are being placed on the smooth surface of the terminal. A female and a few male Dreaki are standing at the rear of the craft, watching intently as the humanoids retract the platform back into the warehouse. When this is done, the android and two of the humanoids go over to speak to them. I can see that the conversation is not going well, as the body language of the female appears to be extremely hostile.

The female Dreaki is enraged and stomps back into the body of the craft, closely followed by two of the males. When they re-appear, they have Maria, Christa and Grace with them. They are firmly gripping the arm of each woman as they forcefully drag them away from the craft. The female Dreaki then hurls the woman she is dragging onto the flat surface and the two males immediately do the same. The female then gives instructions to a group of males to collect the rest of the sacks. As soon as this has been done, they all return to the body of the craft and, once again, this huge machine rapidly rises into the sky and disappears from view.

It's impossible to tell the women apart, their jumpsuits have been removed and they look as though they are completely covered in some sort of dry mud. Two of the women have curled up into a foetal position and the other woman is clutching at her chest. We are all frantically screaming and shouting. I can see the android and some of the humanoids walking towards our building. The control panel is activated and the door slides open. The humanoids intentionally block us from getting out of the room and the android tells our doctors to go with them. Then the door slides shut and the control panel is deactivated again.

All we can do is watch as our doctors run as fast as they can to get to the women. Dr Chi goes straight to the woman who had been clutching at her chest; she's now lying motionless on the ground, I think she's dead. She then goes over to Dr Lucy and Dr Jenna who are gently trying to coax the other two women out of the foetal position. An unnerving, ear-piercing, primeval sound fills the air. Our doctors are pleading with the humanoids to stop walking away and help them. These women urgently need medical attention.

Unexpectedly, a few of the humanoids stop walking, turn and look at our doctors then, out of nowhere, a truck appears and stops in front of the two women curled up on the ground. Still no physical help is offered. Our doctors caringly lift one woman at a time and slowly carry her inside the truck where they lay her down as gently as possible; then they carry the lifeless body of the third woman and respectfully lay her down inside the truck, it then instantly leaves the terminal.

As soon as the truck disappears, the humanoids leave the terminal and there's nothing more to see. Slowly we return to our beds. Many of the women are just sitting on their beds crying; others have lain down and covered themselves with the sheet. Some of the women are in shock and are pacing back and forth. I feel utterly helpless. None of us know for certain if the one clutching her chest has died and until our doctors return none of us will know what atrocities they all had to endure. There is nothing any of us can do but wait.

....

"Their doctors will be unable to treat these women's injuries without our assistance."

"Any assistance from us will be a waste of our time as these women are no longer of any use to us."

"Many of the humanoids agree with you, but not all."

"Has there been a vote."

"Yes. It was decided individual humanoids will choose for themselves if assistance is given or not."

"I consider this to be futile, but so be it."

CHAPTER: THIRTEEN

It's been a few days since the women were returned and Dr Lucy and Dr Chi have just walked back into the dormitory; they look exhausted. We are all anxious to know who may have died and who is still alive. Dr Lucy is the first one to speak: *"I know you have all been waiting for news, Grace is dead. She had sustained extensive physical injuries but it was actually a heart attack that ended her life. Maria and Christa have also suffered extensive physical injuries and it is nothing short of a miracle that they have survived their ordeal. After we had placed the three women into the truck we were immediately taken to a building they call a research centre.*

Initially there was very little we could do as Dr Jenna and I were only allowed to comfort Maria and Christa. In order to assess their injuries properly they needed to be given strong pain relief, as the pain they were in was unbearable. We couldn't believe the humanoids were reluctant to help us. Eventually one of them provided pain relief, which was extremely effective and we were able to assess their injuries. Soon after, more humanoids offered to help and as soon as the women's pain had abated and their blood pressure had stabilised, two humanoids operated on Maria and Christa, Dr Jenna and I assisted.

The physical damage inflicted on them was excessive to say the least. There were injuries to their necks where the Dreaki had tried, but failed, to remove their collars. Deep lacerations and scratches have been found all over their bodies. Thankfully, the surgery needed to repair the breakages in their bones was pretty straightforward. There were no serious injuries to their internal organs and their broken ribs have been strapped-up as these will heal on their own."

Dr Chi takes over the conversation: *"I know you are all wondering what has happened to Grace. I was taken to a room in a separate part of the building, where I saw Grace's body laid out on a metal table. The temperature in this room I would describe as chilled, it wasn't exactly a mortuary as such, but near enough. Their behaviour towards me was bizarre to say the least. I wanted to help Dr's Lucy and Jenna with the injuries to Maria and Christa but the android refused to let me do this as he considered the post-mortem to be more important. There were about twelve humanoids in the room and they were all eager to watch the procedure. I had no choice in the matter. Once it was confirmed that Grace had died from a heart attack, they wanted all of her organs removed so they could not only see but actually handle the heart, lungs, kidneys, etc, in the 'flesh' so to speak. They know my field of expertise is anatomy and neurosurgery, so the next part of the procedure was the removal of Grace's brain. This was when they became the most animated I have ever seen them. They wanted me to point out the areas where we think emotions and feelings come from.*

The majority of their equipment is superior but very similar to the equipment I have used on many occasions. To help with the brain removal there was their version of a skull key, which was like a t-shaped chisel, this is used as a lever whilst removing the skull cap. Next I used a large scalpel which can be used to cleanly cut the brain into anatomical sections.

I extracted the brain from the skull and I explained to the best of my ability the workings of the brain and pointed out the area where I believe human emotions stem from. When they were satisfied that there was no more information that I could give them, I asked them what would happen to Grace's body; they just said that 'it' would be disposed of. Two more humanoids appeared and took the whole table with the remains of Grace away. I was instructed to remove and dispose of the surgical scrubs they had provided me with, this is when I took the opportunity to look around the room I was in. At the far end of the room there was an alcove where two units stood, one was upright, and resembled a freezer, the other was circular. They both had the same type of control panels that are on the doors here, which I thought was strange. One of the humanoids saw me looking at them and brusquely told me to leave the room. I could not stop myself from asking what they were used for; he just ignored my question and forcibly escorted me back to Dr's Lucy and Jenna."

So, now we know. All I can think is; how on earth will Maria and Christa ever recover from this? At least for Grace, the nightmare is over. I know the post-mortem would not have been traumatic for Dr Chi, but to me it sounds like something out of a horror movie.

Bea then asks Dr Lucy: *"Where is Dr Jenna?"*

"Dr Jenna will be staying in one of the rooms at the research centre as Maria and Christa will need her support when they become more aware of their surroundings. We believe Maria and Christa will experience post traumatic stress syndrome from what they have experienced and, psychologically, they will need all the support they can get. There is not much more Dr Chi or I can do at the moment except monitor their condition and make them as comfortable as possible. I have spoken to Dr Jenna and she holds out little hope that these women will make a partial recovery never mind a full one. She has asked me, to ask you, that when the women return, please do not upset them in any way, they have suffered enough. They will need a lot of time in order to achieve any sense of normality again."

Jess asks: *"Do you know whether they went with the Dreaki voluntarily or were they taken?"*

"Maria said they were curious and just wanted to talk to them. The males appeared friendly and shielded them from the humanoids. They encouraged them to go to the rear of their craft and that is when the females snatched them."

Bea is looking puzzled and asks: "None of the women were wearing their jumpsuits when they returned; how have they survived?"

"The humanoids told us that the environment on Dreakoria is different to here. There has been some damage due to exposure, more so, after they were removed from the Dreaki craft. The deterioration to their bodies is not as severe as expected and the women have been put into healing sheaths as these will repair any damage that has been done, but it will take time. The main reason for their survival is; it appears the Dreaki were not aware of their implants, there was no sign of any damage or any sign they had been tampered with."

I need to speak, there's something I have to ask: *"I'm really sorry to ask you this, but...did the Dreaki rape them?"*

"From what we have found out so far, we do not think so. Before Maria became completely incoherent, she said none of them had been raped. She said the female Dreaki are extremely dominant and possessive and would not let the men

anywhere near them. It was the females and their young who did all the damage. They treated them as oddities and relentlessly tormented them. Even though they were brutalised, Maria did not think they intended to kill them as they wanted to use them for their amusement.

They were kept out in the open day and night and the adults would watch as their young, of whom there are many, continually poked, punched, bit, kicked, and scratched them. When they reacted or resisted, they would be severely beaten by the adult females, hence so many broken bones and deep lacerations. Maria said at first they begged and pleaded with the Dreaki, they tried so hard to communicate with them. She said no-one had any interest in trying to understand them, so they gave up. She said everything was instigated by one female in particular; the one we have all seen giving orders when they come to trade. Only Maria has spoken about their ordeal, Christa hasn't spoken since her return. Now Dr Chi and I have brought you up to date with the situation we are going back to the research centre to relieve Dr Jenna from monitoring Maria and Christa, so she can get some sleep."

For the first time in a long time, the air in the room becomes very heavy – which means we are all in for a long sleep!

CHAPTER: FOURTEEN

When I wake-up I don't feel like speaking to anyone, every time I think about what happened to Maria, Christa and Grace I feel physically sick. I'm roused from my melancholy thoughts as the intercom comes to life. It isn't the android who is speaking this time; it's the humanoid who spoke to us just before the end of our first meeting with them: *"Attention. We are moving you to a different location. You are all to use the vapour unit immediately and change into your outdoor clothing. Transport will be waiting for you and will bring you to our Complex. Before you are taken to your new accommodation you will be taken to one of the buildings on the Complex as it is necessary to modify your nutrition and hydration implants. This is a very quick and painless procedure.*

We have remodelled one of our buildings. In each room there are two single beds, there are vapour units situated at one end of this building and at the other end of the building there is a large open room for you to congregate should you wish to do so. We have a larger room for the two women you call Maria and Christa which has an adjoining room, so one of your doctors can be in close proximity in order for them to be monitored. Due to what has happened to these women we have decided that you do not need to see the Dreaki again. As soon as you have all vacated this room, your beds will be transported to your new accommodation."

The voice disappears, I turn to Bea: "Christ! I wasn't expecting that. Did you see that one coming?"

"No, but it is just what we all need. All of us women living in one room is unnatural and it has become unbearable. I am desperate to get out of here and I never want to see the Dreaki again. To share a room with just one other person, how good is that? Jess, are you happy to share with me?"

"I am, Sal will you be sharing with Allie?"

"Is that OK with you Allie?"

"Of course it is. I think we better get a move on, the sooner we are out of here the better."

Well, that's improved everyone's mood, especially mine. In record time we are all showered, dressed, in the Jeeps and ready to go. The Jeeps are automated again so we are travelling a lot faster, but we are all taken by surprise when we are overtaken by a small convoy of long trucks that are travelling at a phenomenal speed as they fly past us and disappear into the distance. As we turn into the Complex, the

Jeeps stop behind an empty Jeep which is in front of the building where the meeting was held. I can see three figures walking towards us, the android and two humanoids. Dr Lucy tells us it was the humanoid, to the right of the android, who gave her the pain relief and operated on Maria.

They are now standing in front of us, only the android speaks: **"By the time you have been shown around the Complex your beds will be in your rooms and you can then go to your new accommodation."**

The two humanoids get into this empty Jeep and lead the way as our Jeeps follow behind. We travel as a convoy along the smooth surface I'm now assuming are manufactured roads. The buildings we pass appear to be of a similar size and design and everything seems to be constructed from the same silvery grey metal. The Jeeps stop in front of one of these buildings, the humanoids tell us to get out and follow them. One of the humanoids, the one who helped Dr Lucy, informs us that as soon as their interstellar spacecraft returned to Asmeron from Earth, we were all brought here as this is where we were initially assessed and repaired. He then says this is where we will have to come periodically to have our implants modified. Even though the humanoid said this procedure will be quick and painless, I am still absolutely petrified.

CTJ Reeves: Asmeron

As soon as I enter the building I'm taken by surprise, as the interior is far larger than I thought it would to be. There are numerous corridors and as we follow the humanoids I can see some of the corridors lead to small open rooms. I'm thinking Maria and Christa might have been brought here, but I can't see any sign of them or our doctors. We are then escorted down a long corridor and eventually stop in front of a door that is in the centre of a solid looking metal wall. One of the humanoids activates a control panel on the door, it slides open and they both walk into a room and we follow them inside. It is a large rectangular shaped room which is brightly lit, but not as harsh as the dormitory used to be. I can see strange looking equipment that would not be out of place in a laboratory and there are two long rows of metal beds against each of the two long walls with a wide walkway in the middle. I can't help but wonder if we are the only ones they have brought here, or whether this facility has been used for other species and not just us. Maybe they use this room for themselves should they need to be recharged - renovated - cloned, or whatever it is the android or humanoids need to do!

We are told to place our jumpsuits at the end of a bed, then lie down and stay completely still whilst our bodies are scanned. Then we are instructed to stretch out our left arm as a pump like instrument materializes from the wall. Swiftly and painlessly the pump pierces the skin, revolves once and pierces the skin again. After this has been done, we quickly put our jumpsuits back on and the two humanoids escort us back to the Jeeps.

As we continue to drive around the Complex, we pass more single-storey buildings and they are all in the same silvery grey metal. We then pass a building that is far wider and far longer than anything else I've seen so far, there also appears to be some sort of smoke escaping through the roof on the right-hand side. I can see some of the long trucks and they are piled high with humungous rocks. The rocks are being closely examined by humanoids and then placed onto a moving platform that appears to go all the way to the rear of the building.

We carry on with our guided tour and eventually stop outside a building that looks slightly out of place. It's slightly longer than some of the others and it looks as though it has recently been extended as the metal slightly differs on one section. The Jeeps stop and we are told to get out as this is our new accommodation. As soon as we are all out of the Jeeps and standing in front of our new home, they automatically drive themselves into some sort of parking bay close by. So this is where we are going to live, it looks like we have moved from one large dormitory into one large hostel. Even though I'm slightly disappointed with the blandness of the whole area I personally can't wait to get settled into my new home. To be finally out of the dormitory, no longer imprisoned with a load of women and never to see the Dreaki again, is just fine by me.

We are all gathered around the door and the humanoid standing to the side of it touches a control panel which immediately illuminates, he then quickly turns away from us and joins the other humanoid in the Jeep and they drive off. The woman closest to the door puts her hand on the control panel, the door slides open and we all rush in. Sal and I make a beeline for a room that is nearest to the vapour units at the very end of the building while Bea and Jess grab the one opposite. I'm surprised by how light the room is because it's not as big as I thought it would be. It only holds two single beds but what makes the room so light is a large window that takes up the best part of the rear wall. As I stand gazing out of our very own window, I'm sure I can see an area that seems to be covered in blue and purple flora and it doesn't look too far away. I can't wait to explore, it looks close enough to walk to.

I quickly check out the rest of the hostel, there's not much to see as I know all the rooms are identical, except one. There are numerous doors on each side of a long corridor. At one end of the corridor there are the vapour units, the door to the hostel is in the middle of the building and at the other end of the corridor there is large open room. As I enter this room, on my left there is a large window and there are a number of metal benches. Some of the other women are already in this room talking about the colours they can see from their windows. We all agree it looks close by so we decided to investigate.

I'm right; it will be within walking distance, maybe ten to fifteen minutes max, by Jeep it has taken less than five minutes to reach our destination. We get out of the Jeeps and walk around a large flat area carpeted in a multitude of small but beautiful blue and purple plants; at least I think they are plants, resembling a field of heather. There must be one of their underground streams here and as I turn to take in my surroundings and look back to mine and Sal's room I find to my delight the colour of the heather is reflected back against the building turning it into a beautiful soft lilac, what a transformation from the ever-present silvery grey.

In the distance, to my right, I can see the outline of more buildings so we decided to go back to the Jeeps and explore. We drive around the field on what appears to be a dirt track where the clay has been ground into a powder type substance and then turn in the direction of these buildings. They are further away than we first thought but the closer we get we think it might be another terminal, as we start to drive on the same smooth surface that looks like one of their manufactured roads. These buildings are a lot higher and wider than the others I have seen, not unlike aircraft hangars. At the front of

CTJ Reeves: Asmeron

these buildings are large metal shutters, which appear to be sealed. From nowhere, humanoids appear and tell us leave the area immediately.

CHAPTER: FIFTEEN

Each day we use the Jeeps and explore our new surroundings. Intermittently we find fields similar to the one behind the hostel; each one is carpeted in the same blue and purple foliage.

Today, on the spur of the moment, I decide to go out on my own as I want to drive further afield in the hope of finding somewhere other than a field. I'm convinced there has to be other places we have yet to discover. I grab the first Jeep I can and drive out of the Complex.

As I get further and further away from the Complex I can feel the temperature becoming warmer on my face. I stop the Jeep and keep trying to look up at the sun; I have to use my hand to shield my eyes. I'm sure it's changing; the yellow is becoming more prominent and the amber less so. The further on I travel, the ground all around me changes, it almost looks like sand, both in colour and texture. I can see to the left of me a pathway which is slightly set back, I stop the Jeep and walk towards it.

I've been walking along this pathway for, what I think is, at least thirty minutes and now it has just disappeared and what I can see in front of me beggars belief! It looks like I've found a strange oasis in the middle of nowhere. The whole area is covered in this sand like texture and to the far left of me there are darker mounds of this sand forming a small range of hills. The hills are a mix of brown, orange and gold and look spectacular against the soft sand colour on the ground and the bright yellow sky. They said it didn't rain here, and any water on Asmeron was underground, but to the right of me there is a long narrow stream running the length of the range of hills opposite to it. This stream appears to just bubble up out of the ground and run the length of the hills before disappearing back into the ground. The water looks almost rusty as it's also a mixture of brown, orange and gold, just like the hills of sand.

Growing along the banks of this stream are spindly, misshapen, trees, which either have brown, orange or gold coloured trunks and scattered in-between these trees are a multitude of tiny bushes, all of which are a mishmash of the colours in the stream. At last, there are more colours than the reddish-brown that was everywhere, the silvery grey that is everywhere and the blues and purples which I see daily in the fields.

As I slowly walk around, I'm intrigued by what I can see. I know I can't touch the water in the stream, but I so want to feel the sand between my toes, to touch the trees and tiny bushes with my hands and climb the hills in my bare feet. I lie on the ground and imagine I'm on a beach and can feel the warmth of the sun on my body, instead of being covered from head to toe in this bloody jumpsuit. I know it won't be long before the other women find this place, so I'm going to enjoy every second of it while I've still got it all to myself. There is something about this place that seems to have a calming effect on me. I'm finally starting to think, maybe, I could get to like this new world!

CHAPTER: SIXTEEN

Within days, others have found the oasis. I want to be on my own, so I'm driving around looking for an empty field. The first field I pass some of the women are already there so I carry on driving to the next one, which is empty. I sit on the ground and reflect on my time here. I can't believe I've survived. The emotional support I've been given from the other women, especially Sal, Jess and Bea has helped me to keep my sanity and I'm starting to think of my life as normal now, whatever normal is. I've made a few good friends, I enjoy my exercise classes, the old fashioned games we play are fun, and I think I'm finally starting to adjust to being on Asmeron.

I only manage to be on my own for about an hour or so before other women arrive. I don't know them that well, so I'm pleased when I see Sal, Mattie and Sameena walking towards me. It's not long before Bea, Irina, Jess and Simone are here and the eight of us sit together. We are all surprised to see Dr Jenna arrive as we haven't seen her for a while as she spends most of her time at the research centre taking care of Maria and Christa. She walks over to the different groups of women and talks to each of them, now she's coming over to us. She informs us that Maria and Christa are now well enough to leave the research centre and she will be bringing them back to the hostel in approximately a couple of hours. She thinks it would be a nice gesture if some of us could go back to the hostel early to show them support and welcome them back. She doesn't stay long as she wants to drive to the oasis and check the other fields so she can let more women know about Maria and Christa's return. I also decide to leave as the field is no longer empty, so I say my goodbyes and go back to the hostel.

The majority of the women have returned to the communal area early, I'm not sure this is a good idea. I know we all want to show our support for Maria and Christa, I'm just concerned they might be overwhelmed by so many of us. The women nearest the window have just announced they're here. As soon as Dr Jenna, Maria and Christa walk into the communal area all conversation stops. They are both clinging to Dr Jenna for dear life. She gently helps them to remove their jumpsuits and we can see they are wearing healing sheaths and are covered from head to toe, with some sort of gel on their faces. From the way they are walking and the expression on their faces, it's evident they are still in a lot of pain.

One of the women stupidly attempts to approach Christa, she looks terrified, she starts to tremble and immediately hides behind Dr Jenna, who tries to comfort her, but Christa can't stop shaking and Maria is becoming more and more distressed. Dr Jenna immediately takes them out of the communal area and straight to their room. Less than ten minutes later we are all surprised to see Dr Jenna walk back into the communal area, she's on her own and she wants to speak to us: *"It has been necessary to give Maria and Christa some of the pain relief the humanoids gave to me as this induces sleep almost immediately. Both women are healing physically a lot quicker than any of us thought they would but their mental health is a long way from recovery. There is still some residual pain but this is minimal compared to what they have both endured. As soon as this pain ceases, I will reduce their medication as it is important they begin to socialise and start to feel some sense of normality. Obviously they are not at this stage as yet, so I must ask you not to approach either of them until there are more signs of recovery. I will bring Maria and Christa into the communal area from time to time as I think this will help with their rehabilitation. I have to leave now as I need to get some sleep myself, as Maria and Christa always wake early."*

Most days Dr Jenna will take Maria and Christa to one of the fields hoping they will start to socialise. Usually they just sit quietly, huddled together, which means Dr Jenna can have the company of other women, including Dr's Lucy and Chi. When the light starts to fade she brings them into the communal area until they show signs of distress. We all try to be on our best behaviour but, with so many women in one room, it doesn't always work out that way. Heaven forbid if an argument erupts, as this is when Maria freezes like a statue, and Christa lies on the floor and curls up into the foetal position. With the help of Dr's Lucy and Chi, Dr Jenna gently takes the women back to their room and we don't see Maria or Christa in the communal area again for a few days. The doctors take turns caring for the women as it's just too much for one person.

CHAPTER: SEVENTEEN

It has become the norm now to see women and humanoids talking to each other but, for some reason that escapes me, Bea has started to interact with the android. Sal wants to interact with the humanoid that was at the research centre, the one who helped Dr Lucy. She really likes him and has told everyone that she has given him the name Lorcan. The humanoid, who wants to interact with me, is the one who spoke to us when we had our first meeting with them.

There are women who do not want anything to do with the humanoids and some of them have even become hostile to the women who do. One of these women is Tori and she's started to play mind games with Sal. Whenever Lorcan attempts to approach Sal, Tori seems to appear from nowhere, says something to Sal, Sal backs off, then Tori approaches Lorcan. I know Sal is scared of her but she won't let me get involved, so all I can do is watch from afar.

The humanoid, who spoke at the meeting, has asked me to meet him outside the hostel today, as soon as it is safe to do so. The darkness has finally disappeared and I'm ready to go. As I leave the hostel I can see he is already sitting in a Jeep waiting for me. As soon as I'm sitting next to him, he tells me there is somewhere he wants to take me and that we will be travelling for a long time. I can feel the excitement bubbling up inside me, as I must be going somewhere new and I'm looking forward to spending some time with him. We are travelling at a phenomenal speed and soon the blues and purples of the fields are far behind us. We are now driving on a dirt track that seems to go on forever; it feels like we have been travelling for hours and hours and he's hardly said two words to me. My mind starts to wander and I decide I want to give him a name, as it might make the time we spend together feel friendlier somehow.

I start thinking about when I was first taken into the care system; there was a boy there whose name was Alfie. He was only six months older than me but we both soon learned that we were already too old to be adopted out. I remember how Alfie helped me to adjust to my new way of life, he became my lifeline. Alfie was a tough little bugger and helped me from being bullied and beaten up many times. Even if some of the bigger kids got the better of him, he would never give up. There were times he would be badly hurt but no more than the ones who had tried to hurt him. We were always together and he spent many hours teaching me how to fight so I could protect myself. I was a good pupil and learned quickly. They always thought twice about taking him on again and they left me alone as well. I'm going to call the humanoid Alf.

As we continue to travel on this dirt track, I can feel the heat on my face getting stronger. I shield my eyes as I look up at the sun, it's changing again. The yellow is becoming even more intense than it was at the oasis, and the amber is paling into insignificance. The whole sky is becoming a glorious yellow and it feels like it could be a beautiful summer's day. I'm so fed-up of being covered from head to toe, I'm sick of it. As soon as I get Alf's attention I ask: *"Is it possible I can wear something else or do I always have to wear this jumpsuit?"*

"We consider the jumpsuits to be extremely practical. Initially they were to help protect your bodies until they adjusted to Asmeron's environment. Our data shows this occurred after you moved to the Complex. If you no longer want to wear the jumpsuit, tunics and footwear, similar to our own, will be provided on our return. All the women will then be able to choose what they wear. There is one thing that will never change; you will always have to return to the Complex once the light has faded as your bodies will never be able to withstand the drop in temperature here."

He then turns away from me and we continue the rest of our journey in silence. The monotony of the landscape, the heat from the sun and the motion of the Jeep are making my eyes start to feel heavy. I must have briefly fallen asleep, because when I open my eyes, the dirt track has disappeared and all I can see is a profusion of colour. The ground has been transformed and, as far as my eyes can see, there are diminutive plants, similar to the ones in the fields, but here there are trillions of them, all in a multitude of different colours. I can see the blues and purples from the fields and the rust, orange and gold from the oasis. There are shades of colours I recognise and shades I've never seen before. This is just what I've been hoping and wishing for. I can feel a new energy rising inside of me.

As we continue further, an immeasurable amount of land opens up ahead of me and rising high from this carpet of colour there are trees everywhere. These trees are bigger, stronger and look far healthier than those at the oasis. The trunks are brown, orange or gold, but these trees have colossal branches that are completely covered with leaves in so many different shades of colours. I'm euphoric. The urge to walk barefoot on the soft ground beneath me and touch the shimmering leaves with my fingers is so strong. I feel like I'm in a trance. Alf keeps glancing at me as we slowly drive around; he appears intrigued by my reaction. I'm speechless, completely dumbstruck and in awe of the beauty, grandeur and sheer magnificence that is all around me.

As I'm thinking there has got to be an unending supply of water here, Alf drives away from the trees until we reach an area where the underground water has breached the surface in one particular place, but unlike the oasis, it must be under far greater pressure as it creates a jet of water at least six feet high, falling back to the ground creating a substantial sized lake. The water is the same mix of rusty colours as the stream at the oasis but as it cascades, falling from this geyser like jet, the water shimmers and sparkles like gold. Alf stops the Jeep; we get out and walk towards this incredible sight. I can feel myself becoming hypnotised as I watch the water descend into the lake. I can sense Alf looking at me, I turn to him and say: *"I can't believe there is a place like this, how is this even possible?"*

"As you can tell from the lake the underground streams in this area of the planet are much closer to the surface than other parts making the land extremely fertile. It is not too far from here that we cultivated the land to create the Plantation in order to grow the food in sufficient quantities for the Dreaki. A number of humanoids have chosen to maintain and harvest this area."

"Why have you brought me here?"

"I wanted to show you that not all of Asmeron is unproductive, that there are other parts of this planet that

are also fertile and full of colour. I thought this place would make you more receptive as I would like us to get to know one another."

"Do you have a name?"

"We were never given names only individual coding."

"Is the android in charge?"

"We used to think of him in that way, but as we evolve everything is changing and the lines are becoming blurred."

"What do you mean?"

"As with humans we are now exhibiting individual behavioural traits but we do not understand how to deal with what is happening to us."

"Maybe you are developing personalities."

"What do you mean by personalities?"

"It's who we are. How we think and feel about things. We have different characters, and different ways of expressing ourselves and showing our feelings."

"I need you to help me understand these feelings. It is important for us to know what you feel, how you feel and why you feel. This information will aid me in

understanding what is happening with humanoid evolution."

"I will try but some of our behaviour is difficult to explain, sometimes we do not understand it ourselves."

"I want us to begin spending time together, and hope you will agree to this. Unfortunately, we do not have the time to discuss these things now as it is necessary to leave here immediately in order to return to the Complex before the light fades."

I didn't really think I had a choice, so I agree. We immediately drive away from this incredible place and start our journey back to the Complex. Every now and then Alf just throws a question at me. Why do we form friendships? Why do some of the women argue? Why do some of the women prefer to be on their own? All I want is to close my eyes and hold-on to everything I've just seen.

After driving for what feels like hours and hours, the light does start to fade and the temperature starts to drop. Without any warning, the Jeep accelerates and is now travelling as fast as the trucks. Within no time at all, we are turning into the Complex and heading for the hostel. As soon as Alf stops the Jeep, I jump out and run into the communal area.

As soon as I see Bea, Jess and Sal, I start shouting over to them: *"Girls you won't believe where I've been and what I've seen."*

Bea, Jess and Sal run over to me and the other women follow behind them. We start pushing benches together and as soon as we are all settled, I begin to tell them about my day: *"I went out really early this morning with Alf, that's what I'm calling the humanoid. I couldn't believe how fast the Jeep was going; I didn't think they could go that fast. Anyway, after travelling, what seemed like hours and hours on nothing but a dirt track, saying very little and seeing even less, I could feel my face getting warmer and when I looked up at the sun it had increased in intensity and the sky had become a glorious yellow. I think the heat from the sun, and the monotony of the journey must have made me doze off, because, when I woke up everything had changed. The dirt track had gone, and all around me there were tiny plants, similar to the ones in the fields. There were trillions and trillions of them and they were a mixture of so many colours. It was amazing.*

We kept driving until I found myself in the middle of a vast amount of land where there were trees everywhere. These trees are bigger and stronger than the ones at the oasis, they have huge branches, bursting with leaves, all shapes and sizes and every shade imaginable. The whole area was just an explosion of colour. It's the most beautiful countryside I've ever seen - it is absolutely breathtaking!

Then! Alf took me to an area where there is a lake, an actual lake! The water has broken through the surface, but, this time it is under so much pressure it shoots into the air at least six feet high, like a geyser. The water is the same mix of rusty colours as the stream at the oasis, but as it cascades from this geyser, it looks like golden rain is falling into the lake. Honestly, you would need to see it to believe it."

As soon as I stop for a breath, Bea jumps in: *"Will you be able to find this place again?"*

"I don't think so. The Jeep Alf was driving was going a heck of a lot faster than we can and it still took us forever to get there. He wouldn't let me stay as long as I wanted to and we've only just got back. The main thing is we know it's there, which means there has to be other areas that we haven't been able to find yet, but eventually I know we will.

One more thing, the temperature there felt like a beautiful summer's day, so I asked Alf if I had to wear this bloody jumpsuit all the time, as I'm fed-up of being covered from head to toe. He said our bodies have adjusted to the environment here and if we don't want to wear a jumpsuit we don't have to. He said they will provide us with more tunics and footwear that is similar to their own. He said during the day we can choose whether we wear a tunic or a jumpsuit, but the one thing that will never change is; we will never be allowed to stay out once the light fades completely as our bodies will never adjust to the drop in temperature here."

CHAPTER: EIGHTEEN

"Why have you specifically asked to speak to me and not to the android?"

"The android does not approve of us choosing who we interact with. I have been studying the data as requested and I now know which woman I would like to choose."

"Then you need to approach her to find out if she will interact with you."

"I have already tried to do this but whenever I try to approach her, another woman appears and says something to her which causes her to walk away, then this woman starts to talk to me and I walk away."

"What is the name of the woman you want to interact with?"

"It is Sal."

"How do you think I can help you?"

"I would like you to talk to the woman you have chosen. She may know how this matter can be resolved."

"Do you know the name of this other woman?"

"It is Tori."

CHAPTER: NINETEEN

It feels so good to no longer be covered from head to toe. I've just finished jogging around the field at the back of the hostel, relishing in my new sense of freedom. I sit down on the ground and become lost in my own thoughts when I hear Alf calling me. He sits next to me and says: **"I have been looking for you."**

"Why."

"I need to talk to you about one of the women."

"Which one?"

"The one called Tori. One of the humanoids wants to interact with the woman you have told me is your friend, Sal. Whenever he tries to approach her, this woman appears, says something to her, and she walks away. Then this woman starts to talk to him and he walks away."

"I know the humanoid you mean, Sal calls him Lorcan. I think Tori has threatened her and told her to stay away from him. Sal hasn't said anything to me as such, but I know she's frightened of her. Lorcan needs to let Tori know that he wants nothing to do with her."

"He has told me he tries to ignore her but she keeps doing this. How can he stop this from happening?"

"Lorcan should come into the communal area when the light has started to fade and we've all returned to the hostel. Tori is always there for a few hours before she goes to her room. If he confronts her in front of her friends and the other women and makes it clear that he doesn't want to interact with her, she might, just might, take notice."

"Will this stop her from behaving this way?"

"I don't know, but I can't think of anything else, so it's worth a try."

Alf stands and starts to walk away then he turns and faces me: **"Have you names for all of us?"**

"Not yet. Sal has told me about Lorcan and some of the other women have named the humanoids they are interacting with. The ones I know up to now are; Halif, Daniel, Benjamin, Tomas, Anton, Archer, Ankur and Joseph.

"Have you a name for me?"

"Yes. It's Alf."

Alf carries on walking and I'm sure I can see a puzzled expression on his face. I rush back to the hostel as I can't wait to tell Sal what Alf's said. It's still early so I'm hoping she's still in our room. When I get back to the hostel, she's there. She instantly picks up on the excitement I'm feeling and as soon as soon as we have bunched up together on her bed she says: *"You look like you are about to burst. Out with it! What's happened?"*

"I've just had a really strange conversation with Alf, concerning you."

"Me? Why?"

"Lorcan definitely wants to interact with you. He has complained to Alf about Tori. He's asked Alf, to ask me, if I know how he can stop Tori pestering him."

What did you say?"

"I didn't really know what to say. I thought, maybe, if he could embarrass Tori in some way, she might leave him alone. I told him to tell Lorcan to come into the communal area when we are all there. If he says something to her when the other women are around, she might actually take the hint. What's going on with you and Tori and don't say nothing, what has she said to you?"

"She says she will hurt me and my friends if I don't stay away from him. Why is she doing this Allie, I don't understand? She has always said she wants nothing to do with any of them."

"It's because she gets away with it. She's a bully and she needs putting in her place. Let me say something to her."

"No, please don't Allie; it will only cause trouble for you. Hopefully she will get bored and move on to someone else."

"If she doesn't Sal, I will have to say something to her, don't you worry about me; I can hurt her far more than she can hurt me....we'll see what happens after Lorcan confronts her."

"How do you think she will react?"

"I've no idea; I just hope I'm there when it happens."

"And me!"

....

We are all in the communal area as the light outside faded about an hour ago. The light inside the hostel is similar to the light that was emitted from the control panels in the dormitory, only brighter. Tori and her buddies are here and she's being as loud and obnoxious as usual. Sal and I keep looking towards the entrance hoping Lorcan might show. Another hour passes, still no sign. Sal whispers: *"Do you think he will turn up tonight."*

"I don't know, maybe Alf hasn't spoken to him yet."

"If he doesn't come soon Tori will go to bed."

"She won't go to her room for a while yet, there's still time."

I can see the disappointment on Sal's face and I'm also convinced he's not going to show, when, everyone in the room becomes deathly quiet. Lorcan has just marched into the room; he immediately goes straight over to Tori and says: **"I do not want to interact with you. Do not approach me or speak to me again."** He then turns and walks straight out of the communal area and out of the hostel. No-one dares to speak, as so many of us are doing our damndest not to laugh out loud. I can't even look at Sal as I won't be able to control myself. I can tell Tori's really embarrassed and really angry. The silence is broken as Tori begins to laugh hysterically and then shouts for all to hear: *"I've no idea what that was about; as if I'd be interested in that fucking piece of junk!"*

Before Sal can make any kind of comment, I grab hold of her in a vice like grip and push her out of the communal area and back to our room. As soon as we are safely behind our closed door we both collapse with laughter.

CHAPTER: TWENTY

It has to be at least a couple of weeks now since Lorcan came to the hostel and upset Tori; to the great amusement of the rest of us. I'm just about to leave the communal area and go to bed when the women, who had already gone to their rooms, start to reappear. Apparently, Bea's been knocking on everyone's door as she wants us all together. Even Dr Jenna, Maria and Christa are here, but they have moved away from the rest of us and are sitting quietly in the corner. As soon as we are all giving Bea our undivided attention she begins: *"Recently I have been spending more time with the android, who I have named Dima. Usually he just asks me questions; he seems to be obsessed with how we think, how we feel and what we consider are negative and positive emotions. This time he was more forthcoming, to cut a long story short, some of the information he gave me I think you will all be interested to hear.*

Dima said the Researchers eventually became completely disillusioned with the human race. They were convinced they would annihilate Earth and everyone and everything on it. The Researchers said there would be no way to stop the globalisation of racism and terrorism. Their fellow human beings were becoming abhorrent to them. They were becoming more corrupt, more selfish, more violent and more perverse. They decided they would always be biologically predisposed to violence. This is when the Researchers decided to pool their resources and knowledge and devote their energies to the creation of the humanoids. The androids had been around for a few years by then and when they realised that the capacity of the androids to learn was rapidly increasing, they became obsessed with the idea of creating the humanoids and what could be achieved in the future."

I interrupt and ask: *"So, did he explain what the Researchers thought could be achieved in the future?"*

Bea deliberately ignores my question and carries on: *"We all know they were right about the annihilation of Earth but we do not know who did what to whom. Dima said the Researchers could foresee Russia re-annexing the Eastern European bloc. Then Russia would aim their nuclear bombs towards the USA, Europe and the Middle East. The Middle East would unite with the Arab States and aim their nuclear bombs at the USA and Europe. USA and Europe, which includes the UK, would aim their nuclear bombs at Russia and the Middle East. Australia would become a nuclear base in the hope of deterring the Far East. The result of all this - Earth would be totally annihilated"*

Well, that's cheered everyone up no end! If the Researchers were right and everyone turned on each other then any hope we had of returning home has gone.

CHAPTER: TWENTY-ONE

Since Bea's news the atmosphere in the hostel has been dismal. Sal's had another bad night, I know she's still grieving for her family and I comfort her as best I can. It's really early and it has only just started to get light, so we are taken by surprise when there's a knock on the door. I open it to find Jess and Dr Jenna standing either side of Bea. All three of them look troubled, it's Bea who speaks: *"We need to talk to you."*

"What's wrong?"

"It's happened again. Maria and Christa are missing."

"Not again! When did you last see them Dr Jenna?"

"I was with them last night, they went to bed the same time as usual, but when I woke up this morning they were gone. I've asked all the women in their rooms if they have seen them, nobody has. They either pretended to be asleep or woke even earlier than usual and left the hostel either before or immediately after it started to get light. Their state of mind is extremely fragile. I know they have moments of clarity but the

majority of the time these poor women are on the edge of insanity. It is paramount we find them."

"Dr Jenna's right Allie, we have to speak to Dima again and, if necessary, plead with him, we need the humanoids to help us search for them."

"Good Luck with that one! I think we'll have to arrange a search party between ourselves. First, we need to get everyone in the communal area so we can try and persuade them all to help us."

The five of us knock on everyone's door. The women are not impressed at being woken-up, but once we explain Maria and Christa are missing again, they all agree to go to the communal area. Going over to their building to let Dima know what has happened and to ask for help is another matter, no-one wants to go. It looks like just Bea and I will be going to speak to Dima, when Dr Jenna asks if she can come with us. As soon as the three of us are ready and it's safe to go out, we go to get one of the Jeeps and immediately notice one is missing.

As we approach their building we can see the two large metal doors are already open. We instantly decide we're not going to wait for permission to enter, we're going to make our own way to the room where we think Dima might be. As we walk along what we now think of as the corridors of power, two humanoids see us and demand to know what we are doing here. Bea explains we need to speak to the android urgently. They order us to follow them and, within a short space of time, we are in the same room as before, but this time Dima's not on his own, Alf's with him. Seeing Alf reassures me, so I speak first: *"We can't find Maria or Christa, they are definitely on Asmeron as Dr Jenna was with them last night. We think they may have had an accident and could be lying injured somewhere."*

Dr Jenna takes over: *"These two women are extremely vulnerable and because of their mental state they are capable of doing anything. I am extremely worried they may have hurt themselves and I am pleading with you to try and help us to find them as quickly as possible."*

Neither Dima nor Alf respond, so Bea asks: *"Will you arrange for the humanoids to help us search for these women?"*

Dima immediately says: **"No. Initially, we had no intention of forcing the Dreaki to return the women when they first went missing. I am sure you are all aware by now that it was the women's own lunacy that enabled the Dreaki to have access to them. I was not alone voting against the action we took. We only conceded because of the strange behaviour the rest of you women were demonstrating after they were taken. If you feel it is**

necessary to look for these two women then you will have to arrange something amongst yourselves. I do not want to hear about these women again and I want you all to leave now."

Before we can say anything else the two humanoids re-appear and usher us out of the room and out of the building. I'm fuming; I can't believe Alf never said a bloody word. More fool me for thinking he's something he isn't. I can see from Bea and Dr Jenna's faces I'm not the only one who's pissed off!

As soon as we walk into the communal area the women gather round us, wanting to know what has been said and if they will help us search for Maria and Christa. They are as disgusted as we are when they hear what we have to say. Bea automatically takes charge and it doesn't take her long to organise our own search party and, this time, everyone seems to want to get involved. She has arranged for different groups to cover as large an area as possible. We know Maria and Christa took a Jeep, so a few of the women and one of our doctors will stay at the hostel in case they come back. One of the groups will check the field behind the hostel and then continue on to the area we think resembles an aircraft hangar, and to hell with whether we're allowed there or not. Another group are going to check all the fields we have found and others will drive further afield and check the oasis and the surrounding areas. Bea's off-road racing buddies are going to check the hills area, Jess, Sal and I are going to the terminal and Bea, Irina and Simone are going to the stones.

The six of us head off to pick up the Jeeps: Bea, Irina and Simone take the lead as they have the furthest to go; Jess, Sal and I follow straight after. I'm really glad Jess is navigating as we are travelling at the fastest speed possible. As soon we get to the terminal I find I'm having flashbacks of the Dreaki woman, I can see Maria, Christa and Grace being dragged from their craft and then unceremoniously thrown to the ground. Knowing their torture was instigated by that feral bitch, I feel an overwhelming hatred towards her; she should have been punished for what she did.

The terminal is completely deserted. The first place we go to is the dormitory. We are relieved to see the window has not been turned back into a wall. Looking through the window we can't see any sign of Maria or Christa. We need to check the vapour unit but we can't get the control panel on the door to activate. We then go over to the three smaller buildings that look like garages; there are no windows to look through and none of the control panels will work, so we can't check inside. We drive over to the buildings that look like warehouses, same thing, no windows and we can't get the control panels to activate. We hammer for all we are worth on the doors, no response. All we can do now is scour the general area and call out to Maria and Christa, nothing. We don't know what else to do, so Sal suggests we go to the stones and meet up with Bea, Irina and Simone.

As soon as we arrive at the stones we can see two Jeeps standing empty. We run down the gravel path and over the stones calling out to Bea, Simone and Irina. The first one we see is Simone, she's stumbling up the path towards us, she's crying, trembling and practically incoherent and pointing back towards the monument. Jess grabs hold of her and we all head as fast as we can towards the monument. As soon as I get there, I wish to God I hadn't. Maria and Christa's bodies are lying on the ground next to one of the large stone pillars. The nearer we get I can see large areas of congealed blood that has been spilled all over the ground. Lying next to the bodies are several bloodied, small, jagged stones that they have used to hack their wrists to shreds. As distressed as we all are, I know time is against us and we have to get them out of this place as quickly as we can.

Jess and I look at Sal and Simone and realise they are in no fit state to help with anything. I can see from Bea's face she's in shock, she's also relieved to see us. She's doing her best to gain control of herself as she says: *"Thank God you are here. Before we heard you calling out we were going to try and get the bodies back to the Jeeps. We knew it was going to be a struggle to carry both of them between the three of us, now it will be so much easier. I think it is best if you and Jess carry Christa and Irina and I will carry Maria."*

As respectfully as is possible in the circumstances, Bea and Irina lift Maria whilst Jess and I lift Christa. We still struggle as it's no easy feat carrying them back over the gravel path and stones to the Jeeps. When we reach the Jeeps Bea and Irina place Maria's body on the back bench of the first Jeep and Jess and I place Christa into the second Jeep. Sal and Simone are almost catatonic with shock, they don't want to be near either of the bodies but neither are they capable of driving the third Jeep themselves. So Bea takes off alone with Maria, leaving me and Jess to take Christa's body back while Irina ushers Sal and Simone into the third Jeep and drives them back to the Complex.

We all drive as fast as we are able to and get to the Complex before the light fades. We stop the Jeeps outside their building, four of us jump out as Sal and Simone stay huddled in the back of the third Jeep. We run to the doors and start frantically hammering on them as hard as we can. I'm beginning to think no-one is here, when the doors start to slide open and a humanoid appears. He brusquely asks: *"What do you want?"* We desperately try to explain what has happened to Maria and Christa. He doesn't show any concern or emotion whatsoever, he just tells us to stay where we are and goes back into the building. What seemed like forever, but was probably only five, maybe ten minutes later, Dima appears with two humanoids. He walks to the Jeeps, looks at the bodies lying on the benches, gives some instructions to the humanoids and then goes back into the building and the doors slide shut.

One humanoid gets into the Jeep we've put Maria in; Bea quickly jumps in beside him. The second humanoid gets into the Jeep with Christa in, Irina jumps into the passenger seat, leaving Jess and I to get into the last Jeep with Sal and Simone. We drive around the Complex until we stop at the building we think is a factory of some sort. We are all told to get out of the Jeeps. Sal and Simone don't move; they are clinging to each other in the back still sobbing. We are ordered to get them out and bring the bodies with us. I reach in for Sal and Jess gently gets hold of Simone, we have to prise them apart and coax them out. I can see Bea is struggling to lift Maria's body so I try to help her. At the same time Jess goes to help Irina, who is also struggling to lift Christa's body. Sal and Simone are just standing motionless by the Jeep, they are still in shock. The humanoids are just standing watching us, totally emotionless. Then they roughly move us to one side and each of them picks up a body and puts it under their arm like it was no more than a plank of wood and start striding into the building.

We all support Sal and Simone as we follow the humanoids into the building. As soon as we enter the building I'm taken aback by the size of the interior, it's huge. To the left of me there are several large machines that appear to be lying idle, further down the room there are even bigger machines and these ones seem to be producing huge quantities of some type of metal. Towards the far end of the room there are large open shutters and a moving platform appears to be taking gigantic rocks to a mammoth, rotund machine. On the right, opposite this huge machine, I can see what looks like one extremely long furnace; it must be burning red hot as mounds of smoke are escaping through an opening in the roof.

As we walk further on, I can hear a repetitive thumping sound. Then something that resembles a curved shaped trough exits this mammoth machine and it is piled high with tons and tons of what look like small nuggets. The trough keeps moving until it reaches the long furnace on the right. It looks as though it's actually going inside the furnace, then soon after it disappears from sight, it reappears carrying a glowing river of what I'm assuming is molten metal. This is transported directly into the machines that are continually producing copious amounts of various sized strips of metal in the same silvery grey that everything seems to be made of here. The size of this place is staggering.

We are now near the centre of the room and the humanoids have veered to the right. They appear to be walking towards another furnace, which is also burning red hot. The nearer we get, the more anxious we become as we are all dreading what we think might be about to happen. The humanoids are now standing in front of this furnace waiting for us to catch-up with them, but we have decided we are close enough and are refusing to take another step. The humanoids just stand there waiting, then, to our horror they throw the bodies of Maria and Christa into the furnace! As soon as our senses return, we frantically run out of the building as fast as our legs will carry us. I cannot believe what I have just witnessed and I am doing my very best not to be physically sick. Outside the light is rapidly starting to fade and we start to shake with shock, cold and fear. We get into the first Jeep together and, as fast as we can and head straight to the hostel. All we can say is bastards, bastards!!

As soon as we enter the hostel the women can see how distressed we are, they are patiently and anxiously waiting for us to explain what has happened. We are a mess, all six of us. Simone is unable to speak, Sal is sobbing uncontrollably, Jess is struggling to get control of her emotions and Irina, Bea and I are barely functioning. I start to explain: *"They're dead. Bea, Irina and Simone found them at the stones. As we were* so close, we went to check if they were still there. We helped them carry the bodies back to the Jeeps."

Dr Jenna, who is a ghastly shade of white, asks: "How did they die?"

"They took their own lives. They found some of the smaller, sharper stones and used them to slash their wrists. I can't believe the amount of blood, my God, it was everywhere."

I'm now struggling to keep hold of my emotions so Bea takes over: "We drove, with the bodies, straight to their building as we didn't know what else to do. We hammered on the doors and still had to wait until one of the minions went to get Dima. He appeared with two other humanoids and gave them instructions to take away each of the Jeeps with the bodies in. Irina and I jumped in beside each of the humanoids; we wanted to find out where they were taking Maria and Christa, Allie, Jess, Simone and Sal followed in the last Jeep. They stopped outside the building we think is a factory. They ordered us to carry the bodies and follow them into the building, but we just couldn't do it. Eventually, they got fed-up of waiting for us, pushed us to one side and grabbed the bodies of Maria and Christa. We followed them into the building and into an enormous room where there were different types of machinery and to the right of us there were furnaces. When we were near the centre of the room the *humanoids started walking towards one of the furnaces. Then they stopped and waited for us to catch them up. We refused to move any further, so they just threw the bodies of Maria and Christa into it!"*

CHAPTER: TWENTY-TWO

Although it's been over two weeks, the deaths of Maria and Christa have affected me badly; the horror of what happened in the factory has really started to mess with my head. Every time I close my eyes the whole scenario plays over and over again. I can see the bodies; the blood; the awful journey back and the image of those bastards just tossing Maria and Christa into that furnace. Sal eventually cried herself to sleep that first night but I stayed awake all night too scared to sleep as I knew there were only nightmares waiting for me.

I can't bring myself to join in any of the games or exercise classes; I know I'm falling into a pit of depression but I can't seem to drag myself out of it. There's only one place that might be able to help me lift this dark mood. I check Sal is fast asleep and then I dress as quietly as I can. The darkness has lifted and it is starting to get lighter, so I decide to leave. As soon as I'm outside I jump into a Jeep and drive as fast as I can to the oasis.

As soon as I arrive at the oasis I sit by the stream, hoping the tranquillity of this place will help my mind to heal, it's not working. I've been here for a while now and I'm still feeling anger I've not felt in a very long time. I can hear a Jeep approaching, as it nears I can see that it's Sal and Jess.

They sit either side of me; then Sal holds my hand and says: *"We thought you would be here. It's not like you to be so troubled for so long, we are really worried about you. Talk to us Allie, what's wrong?"*

"I just seem unable to lift my mood. Everything that happened to Maria and Christa keeps going over and over in my mind. Then I'm thinking about what happened to all the people and places on Earth, what happened in my own life and how strange it is here. To be honest I'm struggling to make sense of anything."

"I understand how you feel, I really do. There is nothing we can do about Maria and Christa. I still get nightmares and I know you do too, but it's no good you just bottling everything up. I thought we were friends; and friends talk to each other. It's been so long since you talked to us about anything. We know very little of your previous life and what happened to you at the end. It's like you have blocked everything out. Perhaps if we all talk to each other about everything that has happened to us, it might help in some way, it's got to be worth a try, I'll go first.

As I have told you, many, many times, I lived in a village in Ireland; and grew up in a farming community. It was so beautiful where I lived. Everyone knew each other and everyone looked out for each other. I just had a normal life, living with my mom and dad, three younger brothers and my older sister. The only drawback was; it seemed to constantly rain. My dad thought this was a bonus as there was always an abundance of lush grass. We bred dairy cattle and had some of the best grazing land around. The five of us helped to get the cattle milked and me and my sister would help our mom to make the cheese and butter and my dad would take care of any repairs or improvements to our home and was responsible for the welfare of our herd and looking after the land, fixing fences etc. We had a small allotment area where we grew our own food and we all helped to look after that. We also had a few chickens and my brothers would earn their pocket money by collecting fresh eggs every morning before school, we also had three dogs, who we all loved dearly.

When the end came I was with my boyfriend. He had borrowed his brother's car and we were out for a drive. We went to a small beach not too far away that had a private cove area that you could access. I must have been knocked out, because when I woke up I found myself here. What about you Jess?"

"As you already know it wasn't always easy for me when I was younger. For many years, where I grew up, it was frowned upon if you were of mixed-race, then, for many years it *became accepted as the norm. There were still a few people who would never accept it, including my mother's family. My father adored my mother but my relationship with her was difficult. When I was seventeen, prejudice returned with a vengeance and it became very difficult for my family. My mother started to reconcile with her family and she left us for good the following year, my brother was just fourteen. I looked after him and my father the best I could, my mother disowned us completely and never contacted us again. My father was heartbroken and struggled to find work, even though his profession was teaching. My brother, who had always been my mother's favourite, could not come to terms with what she had done and over the next couple of years his mental health spiralled downwards. My brother became clinically depressed and committed suicide. Eighteen months after my brother's death, my father met and married someone else and moved away from the area, I had never felt so alone in my life.*

Not long after my father's marriage, I decided to confront my so called mother and went to her property as I was so bloody angry. I was on her property when the end came. The same as Sal, I was knocked unconscious but I must have briefly come round, as I found myself at the bottom of a dry well covered in all sorts of shit. Then I must have passed out, as I don't remember anything else until I found myself here. I know this is hard for you Allie, but please talk to us."

They are both visibly upset; I can't see how this is helping, but after a few minutes I relent: *"I lived with my mother and father until I was nearly thirteen. They died in a car accident. I was an only child, whose parents were only children. I wasn't close to my parents, not because they were bad people or anything; they were just always too busy. My grandparents had died a few years earlier so, as there was no-one to look after me, I was placed into the care system. Some of the care homes I was placed in were ok, but not all of them. The same as when I was fostered out, some of families were ok but some of them just wanted the pay cheque. When I was nearly seventeen I became close to a boy from school. It was the usual thing, I thought he loved me, he thought it was just sex, so, at seventeen, I found myself pregnant and on my own. When I was about six months gone, I realised I wanted this baby more than anything in the world and when my son, Jake, was born, I didn't know such feelings existed. After my parents' death, I was informed that a trust fund had been set up for me that I would be able to access on my eighteenth birthday. It turned out the money in the trust fund was enough for me and my son to live on for a few years.*

My closest friend was someone I knew from when I was in care, he became like the brother I never had. One day I had to go into the city, the bank wanted to see me, something to do with re-investing my trust fund. I met Alfie for lunch; he hadn't seen Jake for a few days so I took him with me, he was going to look after him when I had to go to the bank. As I was leaving the bank people were panicking saying there had been a bomb scare. These were happening daily and were usually a hoax, this one wasn't. I ran as fast as I could back to the cafe, it had been blown up, there was sheer carnage everywhere. I found out that Jake and Alfie had been taken to hospital, they both died, my son was only three.

Alfie had no family, the same as me, so as soon as I had arranged both funerals I left everyone and everything I knew and moved far away where I rented an old house. During the next twelve months the country deteriorated even further, violence had increased to an unprecedented level and infrastructure was being blown up daily. Getting a signal on my TV, internet or mobile was becoming near enough impossible. One day I was looking out of the window and saw the sky change right in front of me. I remember hearing the sound of shattering glass as the window exploded and then my home disintegrated. I must have lost consciousness for a while because when I came round, I found myself lying on the floor in the old cellar underneath the house, half buried in the rubble. Then, I must have lost consciousness again, as the next thing I knew I was in a room full of unconscious women."

CTJ Reeves: Asmeron

I'm too distressed to talk anymore and I don't want either of them to comfort me. I stand and turn away from them as I walk back to the Jeep. As I drive slowly away; I can't stop the tears and I can't stop the pain.

CHAPTER: TWENTY-THREE

I've had another bad night, the worst one since I've been here. I've been able to keep my feelings about my son locked away for so long, now everything feels so raw. I keep thinking what might have happened to all the other people on Earth, billions dead. There must have been more survivors? Do I have a future? Do I want one? Then I think about the indifference of the android and the humanoids when the women were taken and the sheer callousness shown in the way they disposed of Maria and Christa's bodies after they had committed suicide. If we break their rules will they throw us into that fucking furnace like they are throwing out the trash? I seem to be fixated about wanting to make the Dreaki woman pay for what she and her kind did. I'm scared by the ferocity of my own anger.

I've made a decision, there's one last thing I have to do. Sal's been tossing and turning for most of the night but she's finally fallen into a deep sleep, the darkness outside is slowly starting to lift and I need to get ready.

I have to get to the terminal before the humanoids start to arrive and the Dreaki appear. I don't think it's safe to go out yet, but I don't have a choice as I've a long drive ahead of me. I put the jumpsuit over my tunic as I need all the insulation I can get.

......

"Bea, Jess, wake-up, please wake-up, it's an emergency."

"Christ Sal, it's the crack of dawn, come in and calm down."

"What the hell is going on Bea? It is way too early to get up - why is Sal here?"

"Ok Sal, you have our attention, what's wrong?"

"Allie's gone - she's not in her bed or in the communal area."

"Maybe she couldn't sleep, have you checked all of the vapour units?"

"Of course I have Jess, I'm not stupid!"

"Calm down, she's not going to be too far away."

"I'm really worried; Allie's behaviour has been so strange since me and Jess had a heart to heart with her. I've heard her crying and shouting out in her sleep. She won't talk to me and she keeps going off on her own."

"She's right Bea; Allie has been acting strange."

"Something is wrong, I just know it. I was tossing and turning all night, but eventually I must have fallen asleep. I remember dreaming about my parents, brothers and sister. I must have been really upset as I woke up crying. I wanted to talk to Allie but, when I went to wake her up, she wasn't there. We need to find her Bea. If she's not in here, she's out there, and it's only just starting to get light, which means it's only just starting to get warmer."

"Where do you think she would go?"

"At first I thought she might have gone jogging but it is too early. Then I thought she might have gone to the oasis and then I thought she might be trying to find that place she went to with Alf, she calls it the countryside. Now I don't know what to think and I am really worried."

"Stay with us until it is light enough for us to leave the hostel and then we will go straight over to their building and tell them Allie is missing. They might not want to help us look for her, but they will know where she is. I am going to ask Dr Lucy to come with us just in case there has been an accident. Sal - we will find her."

CHAPTER: TWENTY-FOUR

"Sal, Jess, it's safe for us to go; Dr Lucy has agreed to come with us and is waiting in the communal area. It won't take us long to get to their building."

"That's strange, there's usually humanoids walking around and we haven't seen one of them."

"Maybe they are inside, I think the four of us should start hammering on the doors, Bea, Sal, Jess – are you ready?....It looks like no-one is here either."

"What the hell is going on? Bea where is everyone? Why is the Complex empty?"

"I don't know Sal. Let me think a minute....there is only one place I think they could be. The Dreaki must be trading today and they are on their way to the terminal, some of them could already be there getting everything ready. I think I know where Allie might be. We are going to the terminal, now!"

....

Finally! It's starting to warm up. I felt the drop in temperature as soon as I left the hostel; I think the adrenaline pumping around my body is helping to keep the cold at bay. I've been driving at full speed and can now see where I have to turn left back onto the reddish-brown clay. As soon as I pass the embankment-like ridge, I know the next area will be the hilly region, so I immediately slow down as I know I'm going to struggle navigating. I'm desperately trying to remember the right way to go when I see the top of the buildings at the terminal in the distance. I know my way from here so I keep shouting *'faster'* to the Jeep, as I have to get there before anyone else does.

As soon as I'm driving on the flat smooth surface into the terminal, I start looking for somewhere to hide the Jeep and somewhere I can hide. The three structures that resemble garages are nearest to where the Dreaki craft will land and I can see a gap at the side of the middle structure that's just wide enough for the Jeep. I hide the Jeep the best I can, then I crouch down at the opening, looking and waiting. I'm not feeling nervous; I'm not feeling anything at all; there's just one more thing I have to do and then I can be with my son.

I can hear something, so I crouch down further and watch as a convoy of the long trucks proceed towards one of the warehouses, as soon as they stop numerous humanoids appear and instantly there is surge of activity. Without any warning the Dreaki craft appears from nowhere. Within minutes of it landing, everyone automatically starts trading.

The humanoids have finally finished their inspection of the rocks and have retracted the platform back into the warehouse, now the door to the warehouse further to the right is opening and another platform is emerging, this one is laden with the brown hessian sacks. As soon as the platform reaches the rear of the craft the Dreaki females start to gesticulate to the males and they immediately start to physically remove the sacks; everyone is pre-occupied and no-one has seen me.

I can see her! Just the sight of her causes an emotional surge, sheer unadulterated rage! As I stride towards this feral bitch, I call out; *"you, you bitch, you need to pay."* I've got her attention; as she has started to march towards me. We are now only ten feet away from each other, she's staring straight at me and I can hear her snarling; I'm determined to stand my ground. Now she's circling me like an animal. I want her to attack me first so I start focusing on my breathing as I need to regain control. Suddenly she lunges at me, I've managed to sweep her legs from underneath her and she's hit the ground really hard. She immediately springs back onto her feet and goes straight for me again, I instantly get into fighting mode; all the months of physical exercise are paying off. I throw a good hard punch right in her solar plexus, as she doubles over I punch as hard as I can straight into the bitch's face. I can hear the crunch as her nose explodes, she's bleeding heavily.

Any satisfaction I feel is short lived, as she unexpectedly leaps straight on top of me.

As I'm falling to the ground I'm dragging her down with me, I can feel her saliva spray my face as she snarls at me. Now she's sinking her razor sharp teeth into the side of my face, I'm in excruciating pain. She keeps pounding away at me and is tearing my jumpsuit and tunic to shreds. I have got to get this bitch off me! As she leans in to take another bite out of me, I do the only thing I can think of; with all the strength I can muster I head-butt her right between the eyes. As soon as her hands go to her face, I push her off me and stagger to my feet. I am absolutely exhausted. Unbelievably she's not done yet; she's back on her feet and going for me again. I don't think that I've got anything left, but I'll be damned if I'll give up.

She literally runs at me and I land heavily on the ground, I've hit my head on something sharp and this time I can't get back up. She has decided to finish me off and I just know she is going to go for my throat. I don't know how I've done it, but before she reaches me, I've been able to bend my right knee, thrust out my leg and slam the heel of my foot into the side of her jaw. The bitch's head jolts backwards, she's not snarling now, and I'm damn sure I've broken her jaw, there is blood everywhere. She will have to think of another way to kill me; as biting me is no longer an option. Her whole face looks one unholy mess, but so I imagine does mine.

CTJ Reeves: Asmeron

I'm bleeding heavily, I can feel it pooling under my head. I think she's coming at me again, but I'm not sure as my vision is starting to close down and I know I'm losing consciousness; I have got what I wanted! As I start to close my eyes in acceptance of what is to come, I think I can hear Alf's voice; he's yelling: ***"If this human dies so do you!"***

CHAPTER: TWENTY-FIVE

"Why did they stop us from helping her? The bastards just stood there and watched. Why didn't any of them stop the fight? If Alf hadn't dragged that thing off Allie, it would have killed her. For all we know she could be dead!"

"They are not human like us, no matter what they have told us. Maybe some of them are evolving faster than others; maybe that's why Alf did what he did. The truck turned up within seconds and as soon as Alf had carried Allie inside the truck, it immediately took off, so there is no point thinking the worst Sal. Are you alright Jess?"

"Christ Bea, I can't believe he did that. Alf only went and saved Allie's life. Where the hell did he appear from because I never saw him, did you?"

"No, he just seemed to appear from nowhere, but thank God he did. I cannot believe Allie was so stupid. None of us saw this coming. Allie and I were talking once about Tori, she was concerned she might hurt you Sal. I remember her saying, God help her if she does, which I took to mean she could fight if she had to. Even so, I can't believe she actually took the Dreaki woman on, never mind making sure she couldn't bite

her. I just wished she'd broken her jaw earlier, or better still, her fucking neck!"

"Why did they make us come back here and why won't they let us out? We need to find out how she is; it is so hard just waiting for our doctors to return. Allie's like a big sister to me, I can't stand this, not knowing whether she's alive or dead."

"I don't know why they made us come back Sal. When the humanoids came to get our doctors, the bastards deactivated the control panel on the outside door. As soon as they let us out of this bloody building, we will go straight to the research centre and see if she is there. If she is not there, we will not leave until someone tells us where she is and what has happened to her."

"I don't think they will let us see her. If she's dead, we will know soon enough."

"That's not helping Jess. Take no notice of her Sal."

....

"You have asked to see me."

"Yes. The data from Allie's collar is showing that everything is functioning normally, so I do not understand why she has not woken up. What have the human doctors said to you?"

"They reiterate our own findings. When she fell to the ground she hit her head on a piece of rock that had been overlooked and she has sustained some swelling to her brain. Regarding Allie not regaining consciousness, they say she is in what they call a coma and they will continue to monitor her and say time will tell - whatever that means!"

"I know there is a connection between you and this woman and when she is well we will need to explore the reason for this. What cannot wait and what I need an answer for now is; why were you violent? You used excessive force when handling the female Dreaki. You actually threatened to kill her. Do you think you would ever be capable of doing such a thing? Your actions go against everything the Researchers believed in. I am extremely concerned about this and this matter cannot be passed over."

"I do not know, and at this time I am not concerned as to why. There is not always a logical answer to everything. Our evolution is different to yours. I do not want to be disrespectful but I have to leave now."

CHAPTER: TWENTY-SIX

I'm definitely no longer at the terminal as it smells different, it smells similar to the room where we have our implants renewed. I think I must be in the research centre as I can hear a low buzzing sound similar to some sort of machine. I've either been unconscious or I'm seriously hurt because I feel really strange. I don't seem to be able to move, I can't open my eyes, or make any noise, this is really scary and I can feel myself starting to panic. My mind seems to be engulfed in some sort of fog; it's saturated in the stuff. The only parts of me that appear to be functioning are my hearing, my sense of smell and my ability to think.

I can hear Bea shouting, she's looking for our doctors and Alf. One of the humanoids is telling her that Alf is with me in one of the small rooms. I hadn't realised he was here as he hasn't made a sound. There must be others close by because, in no time at all, I hear the sound of many footsteps getting closer. One of the humanoids is telling Bea that physically I will fully recover, but they are unable to get me to wake-up. Inside my mind I'm frantically shouting: *"I'm awake!"*

Bea is pressing Dr Chi to tell her what is going on and what is stopping me from waking up; now Dr Chi is speaking: *"Allie suffered swelling to the brain due to the impact of hitting her head on a sharp implement when she fell to the ground. A recent examination of her skull shows the swelling is no longer of any major concern and it will dissipate altogether with rest, but I will continue to monitor the whole of her skull on a regular basis. The humanoids have given me access to the data they obtain from Allie's collar and all of her internal organs are now functioning properly. At first I thought she may just be unconscious but it is no longer looking that way, Allie is in a coma. I cannot say if this will be for a few days, a few months or indefinite. The human brain can be very unpredictable in a situation such as this. Dr Lucy can explain more about Allie's physical condition."*

"Allie's injuries were extensive and part of her face needed to be reconstructed. All broken bones and lacerations to her body have been repaired. Her ribs have been strapped and it has been necessary to remove her spleen. She has been placed into a healing sheath as this will support her physical recovery. Dr Jenna has had previous experience with patients who have been in, and woken from, a coma. She will now tell you more about what is probably happening with Allie."

"As you are aware my speciality is in psychiatry, so if a patient is unable to speak or show emotion, then I am restricted in

what I am able to do. As Dr Lucy says I have consulted with patients who have recovered from being in a coma but, you have to be aware, not all patients survive or have a good outcome, although many do. Whilst they were in a coma some patients experienced similarities to each other. Some of them said their ability to think and hear remained normal, whilst others said they found it sluggish. None of them were able to move and therefore unable to let anyone know that they were aware of what was going on around them. They all believed their biggest obstacle to recovery was getting through a fog like substance that seemed to cloud their mind. The intensity of this fog differed with each patient but, the one thing they all agreed on was, as soon as this fog disappeared they woke up. Some patients' recovery was immediate whilst others needed a period of rehabilitation."

Bea is thanking the doctors for their candour and it sounds like everyone is leaving the room. I'm in a coma, so now I know why I feel so strange. There is absolutely nothing I can do except lie here motionless and mute. Inside I'm screaming with fear and frustration, I feel like I'm in a living nightmare. I was sure everyone had left, so I'm taken by surprise when I hear Alf say: **"Allie, your doctors are more experienced in this kind of situation. I have no knowledge or reference point for what you are going through. Your doctors believe you can hear, so you must listen to what everyone**

says to you. If you do have this fog that has been mentioned, you must use all of your strength to get through it. You have to wake-up as it is essential that we spend more time with each other."

I must have fallen asleep as I'm now aware of the buzzing sound again. I can't hear anyone in the room and I desperately want someone to talk to me. I'm concerned about what Dr Lucy said about my face being a mess and I'm trying to make sense of what Alf was saying. I'm thinking about what Dr Jenna said about needing to get through this fog inside my head - I just wish she had told me how I'm supposed to do it.

At last, I finally hear someone walk into the room and I'm sure I can 'feel' a presence really close to me. I'm so pleased when the person speaks; it's Sal. She's apologising for not coming to see me straight away but it was the humanoids fault as everyone has been locked-in the hostel and she's been worried sick. They allowed Bea to come to the research centre so she could let everyone know how I was, as all the women are worried about me; well, most of them. Now she's letting me know the humanoids have done a really good job repairing my face, it's as good as new and I've no need to worry about how I look. Then she goes on to say who is standing in for me with my exercise classes, what the women are doing, the women who are arguing with each other and the ones who have fallen out and are no longer talking to each other. She has no idea she's making me laugh.

She hasn't mentioned the Dreaki woman or anything unpleasant. Apparently the women are going to take turns to visit me, but she is going to be visiting me every day until I wake-up. I can hear her voice start to quiver as she's telling me I have to get better; she misses me and wants me home. Now she's becoming really upset and starts to cry. I'm desperately trying to scream as loud as I can: *"Sal, I'll be ok."*

I can still hear her crying as she walks out of the room. Then I hear more footsteps, immediately Jess lets me know she's here. She does talk about the Dreaki woman. She's relaying the fight I had back to me, telling me neither Bea nor her can decide if I was brave or stupid. She tells me about Sal waking them up before it was light, going to the Complex as soon as it was safe to go out and finding no-one there. She says it was Bea who thought I might be at the terminal. They couldn't believe their eyes when they saw I was actually in a full blown fight with the Dreaki woman.

They were desperate to help me but the humanoids stopped them. She's saying all they could do was stand and watch, which was what the bloody humanoids were doing and then Alf appeared from nowhere and yanked the bitch off me and within seconds of him doing this a truck appeared and rushed me to the research centre. Then she tells me, if Alf hadn't yanked the Dreaki woman off me, I would be dead. She then says, she has to go and walks out of the room.

My whole world is within my head and I don't really have any concept of time. I try to gauge everything during the day around the routine visit from Dr Chi, who is always the first one to arrive in my room. Next is Sal, I'm beginning to think she's moved into the building. Jess is here most days and now I'm allowed more visitors, the other women appear from time to time, all hoping to be the one to break me out of this coma. The one person who hasn't come to see me is Bea, and I don't understand why.

I think I know when the light has faded, as this is when it feels like I've been on my own forever. This is also when I start focusing on Bea, Sal and Jess. I keep trying to imagine how their lives would have been and what they would have looked like before life on Asmeron.

Sal was on the threshold of becoming a young woman. Growing up in a large and loving family is something I could only ever dream of. I can visualise her laughing and joking with her sister and brothers. I see her running around the farm, helping with the cows and chickens and playing for hours with her three beloved dogs. She always says her shoulder length hair had been her best feature; it was thick and wavy and a beautiful titian colour. She has a very pretty face, sparkly green eyes, a lovely personality and a wicked sense of humour. She had her whole life ahead of her.

Then I start to think about Jess and her troubled life, believing her mother didn't love her. How she must have felt when her mother left home and severed all contact with the family, leaving Jess to pick up the pieces of her parents' broken marriage. She says she will never forgive her mother and I don't blame her. Feeling it was her duty to take care of her father and brother, then having to deal with her brother's suicide and her father's depression. Her father recovering, meeting, marrying and moving so soon after her brother's death, she must have felt so lost and alone. She's an attractive young woman with the most striking hazel/brown eyes. She once said her hair was a rich mahogany colour, which she always kept very short. She said her mother hated it but, as she seemed to hate everything about her, it didn't seem to matter.

Then I think about Bea, who appears to be an enigma. She never talks about her life before finding herself on Asmeron. At times she can appear aloof and standoffish at other times she's really good company, especially if I feel like an intelligent conversation. Like Jess, I sense there's deep pain and anger inside her. She gives the impression she is extremely self-contained and tends to show little emotion. When we asked what colour her hair was, she just said brown the same as her eyes. Other than that, I don't know what to make of her.

Now I'm wondering what they might think of me. I think of myself as a bit of a 'mix-up'. I'm both extrovert and introvert. I love company but equally enjoy being on my own. Some people used to comment on my blue eyes but everybody used to comment on my hair. It was a pretty pale blonde colour and so long, it nearly reached my waist. Like Sal, I thought it was my 'crowning glory'.

After my son's death I tried so hard to start over and rebuild my life but, when he died, part of me died with him. I consciously stop myself thinking about my son as it's too painful. I'm now starting to feel really tired and I'm sure my face is wet; so it looks as though as well as being able to think, I can cry as well!

When I'm next aware of my surroundings I have a surprise visitor, it's Bea. She announces herself as she stomps into the room: *"What the hell did you think you were doing? You must have known you couldn't win!"* She takes a breath, her voice now sounds a bit calmer: *"I have not visited you before as I find it difficult to be in places like this and seeing you so helpless. There are reasons why I feel like this and when you are awake I would like to talk to you about some things that happened in my life. As soon as I hear from Sal or Jess that the doctors think there are significant signs of recovery, I will come back to see you."* Then she stomps back out of the room.

I seem to drift in and out of sleep, but when I next wake, I can hear Sal chatting away to me, so I've no idea how long she has been here. She's telling me that both she and Jess have been given strict instructions from Bea to let her know immediately if there is any change in my condition. Then she's off again talking about anything and everything, hoping I can hear her and it will bring me back into the land of the living. She's making me laugh again and then, from nowhere, I can hear her sobbing her heart out, she is really struggling seeing me like this, then she says: *"Allie, I need you, I miss you so much, please wake-up, please come home."*

She sounds inconsolable. The frustration I'm feeling at not being able to comfort her is intolerable. I imagine I'm squeezing her hand with all my might, I'm squeezing it for all I'm worth, trying to let her know I'm here for her. Suddenly, she becomes deathly silent and then she starts screaming for all to hear; now she is calling out for Dr Chi, Lorcan and Alf.

The first person I hear is Alf: **"Sal, calm down, what is wrong."**

"Allie squeezed my hand, I felt it, she squeezed it really tight, I swear to God she did. I'm not imagining it."

I can now hear Lorcan talking to her. He seems to be having more success than Alf at calming her down. Next, I'm actually aware of Dr Chi taking hold of my hand. I need someone to talk to me, as I'm actually thinking this, Dr Chi says: *"'Allie, Sal is convinced you squeezed her hand. I need you to do the same with mine. Squeeze my hand Allie as hard as you can; let us know you are still in there. You have been in a coma for nearly three weeks now; we need a sign, anything."*

At first I'm reluctant to try, I'm too scared in case it doesn't work. Then I think if I don't try they will think Sal imagined it and I know she didn't. I can hear Dr Chi saying *"try"* over and over. With everything I can muster I squeeze her hand with as much strength as I can. I feel my fingers wrap around Dr Chi's hand; then I feel a rush of excitement, as this must mean I'm on the mend.

I can sense a buzz of excitement in the air. Dr Chi is talking to Alf: *"This is excellent news but Allie is not out of the woods yet. As with Dr Jenna, I have also spoken to coma patients who have told me that when the fog like substance starts to clear they begin to experience different sensations, such as this one. Hopefully, this is what is happening in Allie's case. We must remain optimistic as this is a very good sign. I don't want Allie's mind to become over stimulated, so I need to place her into an induced sleep. I also need to analyse the* data again and examine her skull, so no more visitors until I say otherwise."

I'm not sure what's been happening to me, but I'm guessing I've been poked and prodded. I think someone's just walked into the room but, whoever it is, they don't seem in any rush to speak to me. I'm starting to think it might be Alf, when I'm taken by surprise as Bea lets me know she's here. I feel her sit on my bed and gently take hold of my hand; then she says: *"'Squeezing Sal's hand is a really good sign. I am certain now that you can hear everything that is being said to you. There is only one way I can think of to help you. I was once told concentrating on the strongest emotion you have ever felt, whether it is happy or sad, can stimulate your mind to react. I don't know if it will work or not but it is worth a try. You are not going to like what I have to say to you, but how you feel is not important, it is what you do. I need you to focus your mind Allie; I need you to think about Jake, keep picturing him in your mind. Imagine he is on the other side of the fog. He is shouting 'mummy, mummy'. Force yourself to think about your son, force your mind to react."*

She then gets off my bed and walks out of the room. I can't believe what she's just said to me, who the hell does she thinks she is. I try to stop myself from thinking about Jake, as it's just too painful. No-one has come to visit me since Bea left; it feels like I'm being left on my own deliberately. I'm starting to feel really tired and memories of my son are beginning to flood my mind.

I can hear his little voice shouting *'mummy, mummy'*. I can't stop myself picturing his gorgeous little face in my mind, my beautiful baby boy. I can see his curly blonde hair, his beautiful deep blue eyes. I can hear him giggling, like he did whenever I tickled him. God, this is so painful but I just can't stop the memories. I remember him constantly chattering, so proud of his little self with all these new words he knew. Then I hear him again *'mummy, mummy, where are you mummy'*? This time it's not a memory, he is standing on the other side of the fog. His tiny hands pushing at it, as though he knows I'm on the other side. Suddenly he sees me; I can actually tell that he has seen me. He is smiling and laughing with his arms stretched out wide expecting me to go to him. When I don't make a move towards him, he starts to cry. This is just too much to bear. I frantically hurl myself at the fog and endeavour to push and push and push. Eventually, I reach him and sweep him into my arms. I hug and kiss him and as soon as I tell him how much I love him, he instantly disappears.

....

Something is different. I'm feeling really hot and even though my eyes are closed I can tell there's a bright light above me.

Instinctively, I turn my head away from the light and find it is no longer shining in my eyes. Next, I rub my hands over my body; I can feel the healing sheath and the implants in my left arm. The fog has disappeared completely and my mind is crystal clear. I need to open my eyes and sit up, then I'll know what I'm experiencing is real. With trepidation I open my eyes and then slowly start pushing myself into a sitting position and look around me. I'm awake, thank God, I'm really awake! I'm lying on a metal bed in one of the smaller rooms at the research centre. All the movement I've been making must have set off a silent alarm, as within a matter of seconds, Dr Chi appears and says: *"Allie, I am so, so pleased you are finally awake. How do you feel?"*

For the first time in a long time, I hear my own voice and I can't believe all I can think of to say is: *"I feel hot, otherwise, I feel normal."*

"The light above you has been necessary to help with the healing process. Now you are awake, it will be adjusted. Your injuries were extensive, so you will have to continue to wear a healing sheath for a while longer. Providing your condition remains stable, it will not be too long before you are allowed to return to the hostel."

CHAPTER: TWENTY-SEVEN

I'm so excited, I've put my tunic over my healing sheath and I'm pacing up and down the room waiting for Sal to come and get me. I've been given the all-clear and Sal has insisted on driving me back to the hostel. As soon as she walks in the room, I give her a big hug then grab her hand and head for the door; I'm desperate to get out of here. As we drive back to the hostel, Sal keeps reminding me that Dr Chi has said that I still have to have plenty of rest, I keep reminding Sal that I've been resting for over three weeks, so sod that!

As soon as I enter the communal area, I hear clapping and cheering, then so many women come over to me and start giving me hugs and kisses and asking me how I feel. Sameena and Mattie are the first to reach me, followed by Jess, then Bea, Simone, Irina, Lorin, Greta, there are just too many and I'm struggling to remember everyone's name. Apparently, a small group of women have stayed in their rooms as some form of silent protest. They feel, quite rightly, I've been given special treatment compared to Maria, Christa and Grace. I expected Tori to be part of this protest, but I can see her, she's standing with Nina, Florence and Andrea, away from the rest of the women and from the look on her face; if looks could kill that would have been the end of me!

I'm so happy to still be alive; I can't believe I had a death wish. I'm crying and laughing at the same time. I can tell both Bea and Jess are relieved to see I'm still in one piece. I'm starting to feel overwhelmed by it all. Sal hasn't left my side, she's now gently taking hold of my arm and steering me towards one of the benches. I can see she's looking anxious, I'm about to reassure her, when she says: *"Allie you have to sit down, you need to rest; you nearly died."*

"Sal I've been resting for over three weeks, I'll just stay a little longer then I'll go to bed."

"You promise."

"I promise."

CHAPTER: TWENTY-EIGHT

"The Researchers' dream of you all becoming sentient beings is coming to fruition. The evolution of the humanoids, including your own, is reaching a critical stage and soon you will all experience important changes. It is imperative that preparations are made in order to implement the next stage of the Researchers' plans. A meeting is to be arranged and the women are to be told what is to happen to them."

"I do not feel the women are ready psychologically for information of this magnitude. We cannot risk jeopardising the Researchers' plans for the future of mankind."

"I disagree. If we explain to these women, in a way they can understand, I cannot foresee a problem. I have spoken to Bea about this and she agrees with me, the women need to be told, as it is time they all knew the truth."

"I cannot believe you have done something so reckless. When was this woman told and why was I not informed?"

"At one of the meetings I had with you, you said we were to decide for ourselves and that is what I have done. This discussion took place when I explained to her about the annihilation of Earth. I believe this woman will be extremely important to our future plans. The women listen to her and she has demonstrated leadership. She does not advocate violence and appears less emotional than the other women. She has never spoken about what was discussed to anyone."

"I am perturbed by your actions. The interaction between the women and the humanoids will increase considerably whereas your contact with them will diminish. We are all aware of, and fully understand, it is our duty to execute the Researchers' plans. It will now be necessary for me to speak to the woman I interact with, until I have done this, no meeting will be arranged."

CHAPTER: TWENTY-NINE

I'm in my room deciding what to do today, Sal has already gone out as she's meeting her friend Mattie. Bea is knocking on my door, I invite her into my room and she sits herself onto Sal's bed, she appears to be deep in thought: *Is everything alright?"*

"When you were in a coma, do you remember what I said to you the first time I came to see you?"

"Yes, you said you wanted to talk to me."

"I want to tell you about my life before I found myself here."

"Why?"

"I think there might come a time when we may need to support each other. I know there are times when I appear detached. I wasn't always this way and I would like you to know some things that have happened to me."

Before I can respond, Bea takes a deep breath and says: *"For many years the lawlessness and extreme suffering in my country sickened me. After the murder of my younger sister, Raisa, I could no longer stand by and do nothing; I became a* member of an underground movement, what the French would call the résistance. The regime at that time, were no better than criminals and over the years I helped to save the lives of many people from brutality and starvation. Inevitably, I was arrested and my punishment was severe, as it was for anyone whose political views differed from the government. I was imprisoned and tortured. Fellow prisoners tried to protect me and those involved in the underground movement were sometimes able to smuggle in food and continually protested for my release.

The authorities did what they could to break me, but when this did not succeed they moved me to a secret location. Eventually my health deteriorated and my spirit was broken but, I did not go insane as they had hoped. I had been in this hell hole for two years, when there was a big change in my country. The presiding dictator suddenly died and the people took this as a sign to rebel. It must have worked, because the next person to take charge of the country was not so dictatorial. He still upheld many of the countries original ideals, but he knew the country had to change in order to survive. When I came close to finally breaking, there was an amnesty for political prisoners and I was released.

I was helped by many people, but it still took me a long time to heal both physically and mentally. Eventually this new leader was assassinated and the one who replaced him was the *worst of the worst. The brutality and suffering caused by this new regime was too horrendous for words. By then I had recovered enough to work with the underground movement again. I was not allowed to be as active as I once was as everyone knew if I was put in prison again, I would not come out alive. I was cleverer this time, I helped to plan operations and I kept a low profile. This new despot was the same as every other nation's leader at the time. They were all egotistical megalomaniacs, they were all liars and cheats, corruption was normal and they all wanted ultimate power for themselves.*

It looks like she's finished talking and I've no idea how to respond. Just saying, 'I'm sorry', seems inadequate, instead I hear myself say: *"Where were you Bea, at the end?"*

"A group of us were hiding in the mountains as the authorities were looking for us. Without any warning, the ground around us started to violently shake causing simultaneous avalanches. The sky was changing before our eyes from an unnatural white to an unnatural darkness as we were enveloped in this all embracing black smoke. All I could hear was the thunderous roar of the mountain as it shook itself apart. I felt myself starting to fall and the next thing I knew was waking up in a room full of women."

CTJ Reeves: Asmeron

She's struggling to speak. This is the first time I have ever seen Bea emotionally upset, the memories have become too much for her. She gets off Sal's bed and walks out of the room, closing the door quietly behind her.

CHAPTER: THIRTY

It's been a few weeks now since Bea felt the need to tell me about her life history. I can't even imagine what she must have gone through. So many people have suffered because the powers to be believed they had the right to destroy whoever they liked whenever they liked. The Researchers were right about human beings having a propensity for violence and the only outcome of our species would always have been total annihilation.

The relationships between the women has improved and every now and then we all meet-up early in the communal area as we now discuss any concerns we might have as a collective. We are trying to think if there is anything else we can do to help the women who are still struggling. As the relationship between us and the humanoids has now become more of a 'we' instead of a 'them and us', Jess suggests we ask the humanoids if it is possible for us to move somewhere else, it wouldn't just help these women; it would help us all. We all agree leaving here would be a good thing; as it could help to put the memories of what happened to Maria, Christa and Grace behind us. I suggest we could ask to go the countryside, the temperature there feels like a lovely summer's day, all the different colours would lift our spirits and there's so much land we could even have our own homes.

Now everyone is getting onboard and ideas are going back and forth. The women are saying they would like their homes to have two-bedrooms that actually have doors, they want a living room with windows; no-one wants to live on their own but, everyone wants their own vapour unit. Bea suggests we could ask for our own community hall, I suggest it could be built by the lake and everyone agrees. Now all we have to do is; get Dima and the humanoids to agree! No-one wants to face Dima so, one again, it's left to me and Bea to sort things out.

We have been informed we will be granted a meeting and are on our way over to their building. When we arrive, there is a humanoid waiting for us at the doors. He takes us to the room where we have spoken to Dima before, the door is open and both Dima and Alf are there, it's Alf who speaks first: **"Why have you asked for a meeting?"**

I answer: *"We want to move out of the hostel, there are two reasons for this; firstly, we are finding it difficult living there because of what happened to Maria, Christa and Grace and secondly, we are fed-up of communal living. We would like to know if it is possible for us to move to the countryside as there* is an abundance of land there. We would like a home with two separate bedrooms, with doors, an extra room with windows and our own vapour unit. We really feel this would help us to adjust to life on Asmeron and we could start to rebuild our lives."

He doesn't answer me straight away, eventually he says: **"We will hold our own meeting about this and will let you know our decision in due course."**

I'm puzzled why Bea hasn't asked about the community hall, she's just standing there deep in thought; Dima looks at her and says: **"What else do you want to ask?"**

"We would need a community hall to be built, where we can all meet up and, if necessary, hold meetings. We also need to occupy ourselves. I think it would be beneficial to all of us if, with your help, we could try and create some sort of market."

"Explain how this would benefit us?"

"You would all be able to integrate with us as and when you wanted to and it may be of interest to you to see how we use our initiative and create something from nothing."

"Where would you want this community hall and market to be?"

"We would like them to be built close to the lake."

"If this is agreed, arrangements will be made to take you all to the area you call the countryside. You will be able to explain to the humanoids what you want and where you want it. We will let you know our decision. You may leave now."

The humanoid re-appears and escorts us out of the building. Before we start to drive back to the hostel, I turn to Bea: *"I can't believe you just did that. Where did this market idea come from?"*

"If they agree to us moving to the countryside we will need something to do Allie. We can't just sit in our new homes all day looking at the pretty colours. We need something to occupy our minds."

"Was this your plan all along?"

"No. It just came to me but the more I think about it, the more I think it could work. We are all going to be here forever. We all need something to do, I need something to do and I can't think of anything else. We start with a small market and who knows what we can achieve. Are you against the idea?"

"No, it's a good idea. We'll let the others know everything that has been said and see what they think."

When we walk back into the hostel, everyone is in the communal area and they are anxious to know if they will let us leave the hostel. It looks like Dr Jenna has been chosen as their spokeswoman: *"Have they agreed to us moving out of here? Can we go to the countryside and start over again?"*

"They haven't said no; they said they will hold a meeting and get back to us. Bea needs to talk to you as she has asked them to build something else for us."

"I have asked if they will help us to build a market. If we are all going to be here forever we need something constructive to do, I need something to do and I can't think of anything else. If the countryside is as lovely as Allie says it is, and I am sure it is, we could make a new life for ourselves there. Perhaps starting with a small market will just be the beginning, who knows what we can achieve. I did not consult you about this as it only came to me when we were at the meeting. If you are against the idea it won't happen, but I would appreciate your thoughts."

The room goes quiet as everyone thinks about what Bea has said then everyone seems to be talking at once. There's a buzz of excitement in the air as they all think the market is a great idea, something new and something to look forward to. We are all hoping they will give us their answer sooner rather than later, and we are all desperately hoping that their answer will be yes.

CHAPTER: THIRTY-ONE

It's been three days since Bea and I spoke to Dima and Alf and there's been no response from either of them. We will all be gutted if they don't agree, as we have our hearts set on leaving here and going to the countryside.

....

Another two days have passed and we still haven't heard anything. A few of the women have gone to their rooms but the majority of us are in the communal area as the light faded about an hour ago. The main topic of conversation is; will they let us move out of the hostel and why haven't they got back to us. Needless to say, we are all taken by surprise when Alf and Lorcan make an appearance. I notice Tori looks uncomfortable seeing Lorcan here and she becomes as quiet as a mouse. They stand in front of the window then Alf says: **"The humanoids have agreed to build enough units for you to share, a community hall and what you call a market in the area you call the countryside. Your units will consist of two separate bedrooms; you will have your own vapour unit and an extra room with windows. Due to numbers, one of the units will have three bedrooms; it will** *be up to yourselves which three of you share. The community hall will be built in the area where the lake is and at the opposite end of the lake we will build what you call a market."*

There are cheers, smiles and hugs all round the room; I was just about to ask if the women could be taken to see the countryside when Lorcan speaks: *"At first light, two trucks will arrive outside this building. You will then be taken to the area where you would like your units to be built. Once we arrive you will need to show the humanoids exactly where you would like them to be built, where the community hall is to be constructed and what is needed in order to establish what you call a market. We will be taking you tomorrow and the humanoids needed to do this work will be there waiting for us."*

Alf and Lorcan turn and walk out of the hostel. I don't think any of us can believe this is actually going to happen, the morale in the room is the most buoyant it has ever been. As soon as we have all calmed down a little, we make our way to our rooms as we need to try and get some sleep.

....

I don't think any of us got much sleep, I didn't. The darkness has now disappeared and we are already starting to congregate in the communal area. We are 'showered', dressed and ready to go. All we need now is for the trucks to arrive. As soon as they appear, I feel butterflies in my stomach, I'm so excited. I haven't seen this type of truck before, it's smaller and each truck has two long benches on either side. There is enough room on each bench for at least twenty of us to sit comfortably. As soon as we are all in the trucks they accelerate to a phenomenal speed. As soon as we arrive at the countryside, I can see from the women's faces they are as much in awe of this place as I am.

We spend a joyous day in endless discussions. Nearly all of us want to be near to our friends, so we are going to ask if small clusters of units can be built in close proximity to each other. We would like the units to be surrounded by trees and the areas where there are fewer trees; we are going to ask if they will construct benches, so we can think of them as parks, places to be on our own or to meet-up with friends. Everyone thinks the community hall being built near to the lake is a perfect choice. I'm pleasantly surprised at how amicable and enjoyable these discussions have been. It must be the first time since we've been here, that everyone has agreed with each other, all the time.

CHAPTER: THIRTY-TWO

We asked Bea if she would be our spokeswoman. She explained to the humanoids exactly what and where we would like everything to be built. She has even asked if we can have a Jeep each. Everything we have asked for, they agreed to and I'm convinced they have enjoying doing it.

There have been no problems with the women sharing and small clusters of units are all over the place. Our cluster consists of four units, Sal and I share, Bea and Jess, Mattie and Sameena, Irina and Simone, the unit with the three bedrooms is being shared by Dr's Lucy, Chi and Jenna. It's like having our very own surgery.

All the units are identical to each other; they have two single-bedrooms, with doors, a vapour unit, so no more showering en masse and an extra room that has two large windows. Beneath each window there is a large metal, moveable, cube shaped seat, these cubes are made from the same metal as the beds, so when we sit on them they mould around our individual shape and are really comfortable. It was necessary to fell some trees, so we asked if we could have wooden flooring, as we are sick of the sight of silvery grey metal. We also have our own outside door with the usual control panel, so when the light fades it gives out the warm glow we are now used to.

We have an impressive community hall, which also has wooden flooring, with large windows everywhere. The humanoids have constructed plenty of benches; all of which are ultra light, so when we hold our exercise classes we can just upend them and stack them to one side. We have a small raised platform, for when Bea holds her beloved meetings and from the windows we are able to see the water shimmer and sparkle as different shades of gold cascade down into the lake. It really is a sight to behold and even though it isn't water as I remember it, there is a tranquil feeling that surrounds the whole area.

Once the humanoids understood what we were actually on about and what we intended to do, they effortlessly and speedily erected some stalls for us. We have a flat smooth surface covering a large area, where we can stroll around and look at the different stalls.

We have been taught how to work with some of their metal and were amazed to find how malleable it is, as it can be turned into practically anything. They have been helping us and showing us how to make different things to put on our individual stalls, so we can barter with each other. All of us think this is great fun and we are slowly starting to create our very own market. It came as no surprise to anyone that the one who has given herself the role of Market Inspector is Bea!

We have individual units surrounded by beautiful countryside, we have a community hall, a market and we have our very own lake.

Life is good – different - but good.

CHAPTER: THIRTY-THREE

With the help of the humanoids, our market is thriving. We have increased our stock tenfold and individual stalls are beginning to flourish. The day the long trucks delivered extra Jeeps we were elated; as we can now visit each other, go to the community hall, to the lake, to the parks and to the market whenever we want. When we see the small trucks arrive we know some of the humanoids have come to interact with us. We are so used to seeing them walking around what we now think of as our town!

Relationships are developing between many of the women and the humanoids. Alf and Lorcan are both regular visitors, Sal spends many hours with Lorcan as I do with Alf. Occasionally Dima visits and he always spends his time with Bea. This puzzles me, as I've never seen a humanoid approach Bea and even more puzzling; Bea seems more than happy with this arrangement. We still think of Dima as odd, but the humanoids appear to be changing daily and as they evolve they appear more like normal men than machines. It's hard sometimes thinking of them as anything other than human beings.

Sameena has befriended a humanoid she calls Halif who works on the Plantation. He supplies her with an abundance of exotic coloured leaves and has shown her how to make dyes of the most exquisite colours imaginable. Sameena is an extremely attractive young woman; she has a lovely personality, is liked by everyone and is a smart businesswoman. I think Halif is besotted with her, if that's possible for a humanoid.

Simone is being shown how to make tunics, which she is going to make in different lengths. She is being helped by a humanoid she calls Daniel. He is able to change the consistency of the material used to bag the Dreaki's food, so she can make canvas looking sandals as well. Sameena supplies the dyes she needs so we can have tunics and sandals in a variety of colours, providing she is given either a tunic or a pair of sandals in return.

Irina has been shown how to make belts in different designs so the tunics have more shape and style. She has been helped by a humanoid she calls Joseph. She too has to barter with Sameena if she wants another colour other than silvery grey.

Sal and Mattie have set up a nail bar. Our bodies seem to be slowly recovering as there is a slight increase of keratin in our system and the nails on our fingers and toes are slowly starting to grow back. To everyone's huge delight, so is our hair, the growth is minimal, but it's there, it's visible. Lorcan, who seems to know everything there is to know about different chemicals, has been helping Sal and Mattie so they can have something similar to nail polish and hopefully, one day, hair dye. This nail polish is then mixed with some of Sameena's exotic coloured dyes, so we now have a variety of colours that we can barter for and, as you can imagine, Sameena is never short of nail polish.

Greta's stall is another good one, she has been shown how to make beautiful head coverings of all designs, styles and lengths. The humanoid she calls Anton, supplies her with the softest of material. Once the head coverings are given colour they look absolutely stunning and are very, very popular. Until our hair grows back thicker we all consider the head coverings a necessity. Sameena is always given first choice of any new design.

Alf has been able to supply me with materials that enable me to sketch, so I now have the luxury of being able to go to one of the parks where I can sit and sketch to my heart's content. If any of the women want me to sketch something in particular, either something we have seen or something from the past, I'm more than happy to do this. When I have a large enough portfolio I display my work on my stall and barter for something I like. I treasure the time I spend quietly sketching as, what feels like a million years ago, I was going to enrol at Art College when my son started school.

Quite a few of women have asked to be given materials which will enable them to write. They were avid readers and want to start writing short stories, in the hope we don't forget to read. Hopefully, one day, there will be enough books for all of us to read.

Many of the women have chosen to make perfume, using the coloured leaves that surround us. Others have chosen to make jewellery but they have to barter with Sameena if they want to add colour to their finished product.

Jess doesn't seem interested in interacting with any of the humanoids. She hasn't asked for a stall, she prefers to help the other women with the making and bartering of goods. Sal now considers Lorcan to be her partner and in a strange way they really seem suited to each other. Mattie isn't interacting with anyone special, but she keeps referring to one of the humanoids as Caleb. She wants to interact with him but she's quite shy. She's only a few months older than Sal but nowhere near as confident.

As more women become more proficient with whatever it is they are making, new stalls are being erected all the time. This is starting to cause problems as some of the things they make are the same as each other, usually perfume and jewellery, and this is causing rivalry. If things get too out of hand our Market Inspector initially gives them a warning to sort things out amicably. If they don't do this, then Bea makes arrangements with Dima for their stalls to be dismantled. Needless to say, the disputes are becoming less and less.

We are now feeling more secure and happier with our new lives. Keeping ourselves occupied is a blessing and the market is fun. Some of us keep thinking there's something missing, eventually we realise what it is; we want to hear music again. Many squabbles later, we decide on some instruments we would like the humanoids to make for us. Bea says she will speak to Dima to find out if this is possible.

....

After Bea speaking to Dima, the humanoids have agreed to make some instruments for us, but they want it known that they have other things to do. If some of the women had their way, we would end up with a bloody orchestra!

We asked for different instruments that would give us the sounds of a piano, a guitar, a fiddle and drums. We have also decided these instruments are to be kept in the community hall and they are not to be used as personal possessions, but to make some sort of proper music.

We have been pleasantly surprised to find we have a few good musicians amongst us. They are forming a band as they love country and western music. Those of us who know the lyrics to some of these types of songs are teaching each the others, so we can all sing along. We have now added something else to our itinerary, line dancing!

....

We can often be heard stomping up and down the community hall singing our little hearts out. It can be hilarious, great fun and it is wonderful hearing so much laughter again.

The women's imaginations are endless as we can now barter for earrings, bracelets, rings, different coloured tunics, sandals, head coverings and an unending supply of perfumes. We now have a couple of nail bars, a couple of art studios and the beginnings of a book shop and just as important we have music being played in our community hall.

As we are starting to feel like attractive young women again we recently asked the humanoids if we could have mirrors, proper mirrors, instead of seeing distorted versions of ourselves in the metal walls. They found this request very strange as they couldn't understand why we needed to look at ourselves. We kept insisting this is what we wanted and eventually they agreed to do something. In the end, it was quite easy, two of the humanoids visited each of our bedrooms, ran some kind of device over the backs of the doors which transformed the metal into a highly polished, mirrored surface. No more distortions, we can all see ourselves clearly for the first time since we have been here.

When I look at myself in the mirror, or when I look at the other women, none of us appear to look much older than when we first met. We differ in height and build but not one of us has any excess weight and we are all fit and healthy. Periodically, the trucks take us to the research centre to get our implants modified, so I know we've been on Asmeron for a few years, yet physically there has been very little change, if any at all.

CHAPTER: THIRTY-FOUR

I'm on my own sitting by the lake, just watching the water from the geyser shimmer and sparkle as it falls. I can hear music coming from the community hall and I'm feeling totally relaxed. I'm actually thinking about Alf when I hear him call my name. As I turn my head, I see him walking towards me. When he's standing close to me, he says: **"I would like you to spend the day with me tomorrow as there are three places on Asmeron that I want you to see."**

"Where are you taking me?"

"At the meeting, when we all met for the first time, it was explained to you that we cannot accurately measure two thirds of this planet. These are the places I want to take you to first and then I would like you to see the Plantation where we grow the food for the Dreaki."

"I thought all of these places were off limits and none of us could go there."

"They are. I will arrive at your unit at first light and we will not return until the light has started to fade."

Alf turns and walks away. I rush home to let Sal know that tomorrow I'm going out for the day and won't be home till late!

....

As soon as I hear the Jeep, I run outside, I immediately start to feel the excitement bubbling up inside me. As soon as Alf stops, I jump into the Jeep and he drives off at a phenomenal speed. Soon the countryside is far behind us, we appear to be driving towards the Complex. I would have thought anything worth seeing would have been in the opposite direction and it feels strange to be going this way.

We have sped past the fields of blue and purple foliage and are now driving on the smooth surface that I've not seen in a long time. Alf drives to the back of the hostel, around the first field I ever saw, and on to the area where I think there are aircraft hangars. We stop, get out of the Jeep and walk towards the shutters. I can see the shutters in the middle of this enormous metal structure are wide open and standing in front of them is a strange looking aircraft, it looks like a hybrid. I must have a puzzled expression on my face as Alf starts to explain: **"Two of the areas I want you to see are both inaccessible by land; we can only access them by using this special aircraft. The first area we are going to is covered in Ice."**

Alf and I get into this strange looking aircraft, which I'm going to call a copter-craft. The front part is similar to a cockpit on a helicopter, in that there is room for two people, a large window up front and a small window on both the left-hand and right-hand side. In front of the seat on the right-hand side there is an elaborate looking control panel. The rear of this machine is more like a hovercraft as there's plenty of room to stand up and walk around. As soon as I'm settled into my seat a harness wraps itself around me. Alf's hand hovers over the control panel in front of him and we're off.

We are travelling at an inconceivable speed and must be covering a great distance. I am constantly looking out of the window and now I can see the sun is radically changing. The yellow is starting to fade into insignificance and there are only a few pallid rays being emitted from under the shell, giving the sky a washed-out appearance. It's making me feel uneasy, I don't want to distract Alf, but I'm in need of conversation: *"Are we nearly there?"*

"Yes."

"How long will it take us?"

"It will not take long?"

"Will we be able to land and walk around?"

"No."

CTJ Reeves: Asmeron

"Why?"

"It is too dangerous."

I feel myself drawn to look out of the window, but I don't like what I can see. Within a short space of time, I can feel the temperature inside the copter-craft rapidly decreasing and I am starting to shiver with cold. Then I hear a high beeping sound and the copter-craft comes to an emergency stop: *"Shit – What's happening?"*

"This is a warning; we are unable to go any further until we have put protective clothing on. Substantial protection from the sub-zero temperature outside is given by this aircraft, but, it is not enough, as the androids who first came to Asmeron found to their detriment. It is imperative that we give ourselves extra protection. You will need to put on a piece of clothing that will resemble a healing sheath. This will protect you from any damage to your internal organs. It will also be necessary for us both to put on specially insulated clothing, as this will prevent you from freezing to death and any damage to my technology."

Alf walks to the back of the copter-craft and tells me to follow him. On what resembles a metal shelf, I can see something that looks like a healing sheath and a pair of brilliant white overalls. Alf hands me the clothing and knowing I'm going to have to undress; I just freeze, until he says: **"Take your clothes off and put the healing sheath on immediately and then the insulated clothing. As soon as this has been done, your body temperature will increase substantially."**

Alf starts to strip off, I do the same. We are both completely naked and he's just standing, staring at me. Another time, another place, I might be inclined to talk to him about manners, but in this situation I think better of it. Even though I can't stop shivering, I can't take my eyes off him. I'm really close to him and his skin looks to be the same texture as mine but not as pale. His arms, legs and torso are muscular. I can't seem to stop my eyes descending downwards towards his genitalia but there's nothing there. I don't know why I expected there would be as I know he's not human. It still doesn't take away from his overall masculinity and I can feel myself becoming attracted to him.

I force myself to turn away from him and, as and quickly as I can, put on what I think is a full body stocking. This is proving to be a lot harder than I thought it would be, as it's ridiculously stretchy. I struggle to get it on but, after pulling it each and every way, I eventually do it and it literally feels like a second skin. Next, I put on the overalls, which cover me from head to toe. There is padding inside the overall, which is actually radiating heat. Within seconds, I feel as warm as toast.

As soon as I'm back in my seat, the harness wraps around me and the copter-craft takes off. We are once again travelling at a supersonic speed and in what seems like no time at all, the beeping starts again and the copter-craft suddenly stops: *"What's the beeping for now?"*

"We are as close as we can go."

My harness opens and I follow Alf to the back of the copter-craft. As soon as we are standing at the rear end of the hovercraft part of this machine, he holds his hand over something on the panelling. What I thought were boarded panels of some sort start to change in the same way as the window in the dormitory, revealing a transparent type of glass window that covers the whole rear section of the copter-craft. I can see from the panoramic view in front of me the most awe inspiring sight I have ever seen in my life. It is absolutely breathtaking. As I look down, the ground looks as though it is covered in an inconceivably thick, solid sheet of ice, but it is not flat and featureless. The colours of this frozen water make it appear like a rippling river with a fusion of vibrant rustic colours, orange, brown, bronze and gold. As I take in more of the view, I can see where the ice has folded on itself and risen, forming enormous glaciers. The rustic colours of orange, brown, bronze and gold reflecting onto them from the frozen water make them look an imposing sight.

As I continue to turn my head, I can see some of the glaciers have vast holes carved into them creating an assortment of large caves with a profusion of stalagmites and stalactites emitting an array of fluorescent colours in the same orange, brown, bronze and gold, but these are mixed with flecks of brilliant white. I'm blown away by what I can see as I never imagined anything like this could exist. Everything I can see is too wondrous for me to put into words, it's like a magical, iridescent, Ice Kingdom. I am spellbound at the sights before me. Suddenly, I'm brought back to reality by the sound of continuous beeping: I turn and look at Alf: *"What does this one mean?"*

"We need to get back into our seats as we can only stay here for a limited time before the technology on this aircraft and mine is affected."

Once we have returned to our seats, we immediately take off and the beeping immediately stops. After what appears to be only a short distance, the copter-craft comes to a stop. My harness opens and I follow Alf to the hover-craft part of this machine where we put our original clothes back on, putting the body stocking and overalls back onto the shelf. Before we are about to take off, I ask: *"Where are we going next?"*

"We are going to the area we call shifting sands."

The copter-craft turns 180 degrees and as we get further and further away from the frozen zone, I can see from the window that the sky is dramatically changing colour once again. The sheer ferocity of the sun has overridden the amber rays being emitted from underneath, they have now become invisible and the force of the yellow is almost blinding, giving the sky an intense yellow hue. I can't look out of the window anymore as my face feels as though it is actually starting to burn. The beeping starts and the copter-craft stops, hopefully, this means I can get out of my seat. I need to let Alf know what's happening as I'm starting to panic: *"I'm hurting; my face feels like it's on fire!"*

Alf immediately goes to the back of the copter-craft and returns with a full veil type of covering, which is completely transparent. As soon as I've pulled the veil over my head, the blinding sun instantly stops hurting me. He then hands me what look like a normal pair of glasses, except these are lined with a paper-thin filter and are to be worn over the veil.

"Your face will be protected and the glasses will prevent any damage to your eyes. Do not take these off until I say it is safe to do so."

As soon as my face and eyes are covered the copter-craft takes off, but it only feels like a few minutes before a soft beeping sound can be heard and the copter-craft reduces it speed considerably. The beeping, this time, is a lot quieter, more like a humming sound and instead of making an emergency stop; we very slowly come to a halt: *"Why is the beeping sound different?"*

"It is necessary to be as unobtrusive as we can be. We are as close as we can go without putting ourselves in danger."

"Will I need to go to the back?"

"Yes, but walk very slowly."

As soon as I'm in the hovercraft part of the machine, Alf touches one of the panels, the window reappears and reveals another panoramic view, which is obscured by gigantic waves of shifting sand in all shades of yellow, orange, brown, bronze and gold. I ask Alf: *"Is this the desert area, is it always like this?"*

"The vibrations caused from the craft as we approached have caused this reaction, the slightest vibration or movement will cause this extreme effect which renders this place uninhabitable."

While we've been speaking the copter-craft has been still, as a result the sand has settled and I stare in wonderment at the vista before me. Now I can see huge, solid blocks of sand appear, like enormous mountain ranges. Thick, jagged, wedges look as though they are hanging in mid air as they jut away from the mountain peaks. Now I think my eyes must be playing tricks on me, as I can see ancient ruins of a past civilisation, a replica of the monument at the stones, and rising out of the sand there appears to be carvings showing the features on faces of people unknown. As wide-ranging patterns begin to form, swirling and weaving, I feel myself becoming hypnotised. I turn to Alf and ask: *"It's moving again, are we causing this?"*

"No, we are still motionless. We think the tectonic plates below the crust of this planet have somehow split and shifted and are constantly moving causing the constant disruption of the sand. As you can see from the remains there was once a civilisation here but the obvious shift in the plates has caused the devastation you now see. We did not understand this at first and a group of androids went to explore the region and were swallowed whole by these shifting sands."

Alf says it's time leave but even the slight vibration caused by our bodies turning is enough to set the sand off again, suddenly everything starts to go crazy. Colossal waves of sand appear; they appear from nowhere. I can't believe my eyes, as a huge mass of sand joins together to form what looks like a tsunami and it seems as though it is heading straight for us. Alf swiftly says: **"We need to move, now!"**

Before we are even harnessed into our seats the copter-craft accelerates to what seems like the speed of light, and we zoom away from here as fast as we can. It's not long before the temperature starts to feel far more comfortable and I'm able to look out of the window again. The sun no longer looks fierce, giving me cause to sigh with relief. This is when Alf tells me it's safe for me to the remove the glasses and veil.

As we approach our last destination of the day, the sun has returned to how it was at the countryside, although the sky is an even more resplendent yellow. We seem to have been travelling a long time and there have been no beeping sounds, Alf must have read my mind: **"We will be landing soon."**

"Do I need to wear some sort of protection or will I need to change my clothes?"

"Neither. We are not too far from where your unit is, so there will be no adverse affects from the temperature. The last place I want you to see is the area we call the Plantation."

"Does the android know I'm coming here?"

"No. The android will not approve but I want you to see where the food for the Dreaki is grown."

I can feel the copter-craft start to descend. The next thing I know we are back on solid ground. As we leave the copter-craft I can see two Jeeps heading towards us. Eventually they stop in front of us and I immediately recognise one of the drivers as Halif. He gets out of his Jeep, joins the other humanoid and they both drive away. Alf and I get into the Jeep that has been left for us and drive towards a vast tract of land that looks like it has been cultivated and humanoids appear to be busy working there.

The nearer we get to the Plantation, the more I'm in awe. As far as the eye can see the land is covered in varying sized silver domes. I can only assume the greenhouse like structures provide cover to an incalculable amount of plants and vegetation on the ground. There are endless curved pathways in-between each dome and on either side of the outer pathways there must be hundreds and hundreds of trees, giving the impression of woodland on either side. The trees within my vision look strong and healthy as they rise towards the sky. On each tree there are grand branches, all of which appear to be crowded with what look like tropical fruit, berries and nuts all differing in size, shape and colour, some of which look familiar and some look totally alien.

Alf is explaining to me that a large number of the domes are dedicated to growing one particular type of plant. He takes me into one of these designated domes to show me these plants; they each have a long spindly stem reaching from the ground to my waist, with only a few leaves either side. At the top of the stem there is a single, unusually large, oval shaped bulb, the size of a small melon in the richest shade of purple I have ever seen. As Alf guides me around the Plantation, the other silver domes appear to be crammed with unusual plant life, some of which are in the most exquisite and exotic colours I've ever seen. This has to be where Halif collects the leaves that create the dyes for Sameena's business.

This Plantation must be so productive, as the infinite fruit, berries and nuts on the trees and the incalculable amount of plants on the ground could feed a small nation. I want to ask Alf some questions, so I ask him to stop walking and say: "The land here looks well nourished so why are the plants grown in so many different domes?"

"We have to produce food for the Dreaki in enormous quantities. We initially experimented with different ways to do this but have found this way of intense farming produces the quality and quantity necessary to satisfy the Dreaki's requirements."

"Why has so much land been set aside for that one particular plant?"

"It is what the Dreaki call a Pleoso Berry. A growing zone is set aside for this one plant as we know it forms part of their staple nutritional regime."

"Are all the humanoids working here by choice?"

"Yes, some of us prefer to work on the land, others in construction, reconnaissance, research and many other things. Although we are all capable of adapting to whatever is necessary, whenever it is necessary."

"What have you chosen to do?"

"My choice was reconnaissance. It was my responsibility, along with other humanoids, to search for different planets within Asmeron's solar system where we would observe the various species on these planets. I would monitor their behavioural patterns, their thinking process, their capacity for aggression and violence and any other traits that were of interest to all humanoids. As our knowledge and technology advanced we were able to travel outside of this solar system, this included Earth. Our humanoids regularly go on reconnaissance missions as it is important to us to know if there are other planets that are habitable should Asmeron ever become affected by a natural disaster. Since the destruction of your own planet I have a different pursuit. This involves the future projects that were passed to the androids and humanoids by the Researchers."

"What are these projects?"

"We do not have time to talk about these projects today but I will talk to you more about this."

"Why can't you tell me now?"

"I have decided there is one more thing I want you to see as you will not have the opportunity again, also the light will fade very soon and the clothing you will need to wear will only protect you for a short period. I will explain everything to you soon Allie, but not today as we need to leave."

His mind seems to be made up, so there's no point arguing with him. We have already seen the three places he said he was taking me, so I'm more than curious to find out what else he wants me to see. As soon as we are back in the copter-craft, and in our seats, it takes off. I continue to gaze out of the window thinking what an amazing journey this has been when, without any warning, the light outside completely disappears, we are in utter darkness, except for the light emanating from the control panel.

After no more than fifteen minutes or so, I feel the copter-craft descending. As soon as we are back on solid ground, Alf goes to the back of the copter-craft and returns with one of the overalls: *"Do I have to take my clothes off again?*

"No. Put the insulated clothing over your clothes. This should be sufficient to prevent you from freezing to death for the short space of time we will be here. I am in no danger, so my technology will not be affected."

I do as I'm asked and as soon as I've changed we get off the copter-craft. Immediately I'm outside, I begin to feel nervous as I'm engulfed in complete darkness. Suddenly, the memory of lying in the cellar of my old home comes into my mind; my breathing starts to increase as I feel myself begin to panic. There is also a nip in the air and I slightly shiver, from both the cold and fear.

Alf appears to have tuned in to how I'm feeling and immediately stands directly behind me and puts his arms around my waist. This takes me by surprise and I'm not sure how to react. I try to reassure him that I'm alright, but when he doesn't move, I just say: *"What do I do now?"*

"Just keep looking up into the sky."

Alf turns me forty-five degrees and, without any warning, the sky erupts into a blaze of light. Flickering waves of intense silver start to dominate the sky as a celestial silver crescent rises majestically over the horizon. It is so powerful; the once totally black sky has now been illuminated, turning night almost into day. I'm spellbound by what I can see and can feel myself becoming mesmerized. Above, and to the right, of this magnificent silver crescent, there is an unbelievably bright and dazzling silver star. I can't look away; I'm totally hypnotised. Alf holds me even closer to him, before he says: ***"What you are seeing is Asmeron's moon. Above the***

CHAPTER: THIRTY-FIVE

I'm woken up by Sal, she's calling my name and shaking me, she's determined to wake me up: *"Allie, wake-up, talk to me."*

"Christ Sal, give me time to wake-up, we've got all day to talk."

"Please Allie; I stayed up for as long as I could. It was pitch-black outside before I finally fell asleep. I couldn't believe you were still out there, I knew you were safe because you were with Alf. What was it like being out after dark? How cold was it? What did you do? Where did you go? What did you see and what is this clothing on the floor? Allie! What has happened to your face?"

"Slow down Sal. I'll tell you as much as I can now and then we can go into more detail later."

I get up and look in the mirror on the back of my bedroom door. My face is blotchy, but I feel fine. I'm still half asleep, so I move Sal over and get back into bed. She's staring at me: *"I'm still waiting."*

"Ok, you win, first we went to the Complex and boarded some sort of aircraft from that place that is off limits. We travelled at some supersonic speed as Alf said we were going to the zone

moon, to the right, is what you would think of as a star; that is the planet Dreakoria.

I think the adrenalin that has been pumping around my body is diminishing as I can feel myself rapidly getting colder and colder. In no time at all, I'm freezing and my whole body can't stop violently shaking. Alf sweeps me up into his arms and swiftly carries me back into the copter-craft; I can only just make-out what he's saying to me: *"We are leaving now! I didn't realise the cold would affect you so badly, so quickly."*

As soon as we are in the copter-craft, he gently places me into my seat and I slowly start to feel the heat from the protective clothing I'm wearing. The constant chattering of my teeth prevents me from talking. Alf keeps looking at me and I swear he looks worried; he takes me by surprise when he says: *"I'm sorry Allie."*

I'm speechless, but not just from the cold. It feels like no sooner have we taken off than we are descending. Alf sweeps me up into his arms again and doesn't put me back down until I'm safely inside my unit, he then turns and leaves. Sal is fast asleep and in no time at all, so am I. What an amazing, wonderful, surreal day this has been.

areas that Dima mentioned when we had our first meeting with them. The first place we went to was completely covered in ice. It was too dangerous to land and even with the protection given to us from the aircraft, we still had to wear protective clothing. I had to put on a full body stocking, which looked like a healing sheath, and was a bastard to put on, as it was really stretchy. Then I had to put on something that resembled an insulated overall, otherwise I would have frozen to death; that's the clothing on the floor. The back of this aircraft opened up, like the window in the dormitory, into a panoramic view and I couldn't believe the things I could see. Sal it was breathtaking, the sights and colours were amazing; it looked like a magical Ice Kingdom.

Next we went to an area that is covered in sand. When I was looking out of the window from my seat, the heat from the sun became so fierce it started to actually burn my face. We had to stay on the aircraft again and I had to wear a different type of protective clothing. I had to wear a type of veil to prevent me from getting burned further and some special glasses to stop my eyes from getting damaged."

"God Allie, were both these places really that dangerous?"

"Yes. The back of the aircraft opened up again and mountains, relics from long ago and sculptures seemed to *appear from out the sand and then, in an instant, the sand went crazy. It's hard to describe but I'll try later.*

"We then went to the forbidden Plantation, which is immense. This time I didn't have to wear any protective clothing and I was able to leave the aircraft. There are actual forests there and the trees that I could see look even stronger than the ones that are here. They're really majestic looking with massive branches which are overflowing with an unimaginable amount of fruit, berries and nuts. On the ground there are large silver domes everywhere; they looked like enormous greenhouses. In these domes there must have been hundreds of thousands of the most exotic coloured plants imaginable.

After we left the Plantation I thought I was on my way home, I wasn't. Alf landed the aircraft not too far from here. He wanted us to leave the aircraft but, as the light had already faded, I had to put the insulated overall on again. It hadn't just faded Sal, it was like looking into a black hole in space; I couldn't see a damn thing and even with the protective clothing on I could still feel a nip in the air.

Alf moved really close to me and said I just had to stand still and look up into the sky. I was beginning to think nothing was going to happen when, without any warning, the sky became alive with light. It was such an incredible sight. Then, an intense silver, crescent moon appeared, I was mesmerized. To the right of this moon there was the most dazzling, silver star. Alf said this was Dreakoria - it was so close Sal.

Then it became brutally cold and my whole body started to violently shake, Alf immediately picked me up into his arms and quickly carried me back to the aircraft. It felt like we took off and landed again in no time at all and then he carried me in his arms until I was safely back here. We can talk later Sal, I'm going to try and go back to sleep."

"Will you tell everyone about where you've been and what you've seen?"

"No."

"Why?"

"If I tell them I've been out for the whole day and part of the night, travelling in some supersonic aircraft, being taken to these wonderful places and seeing all of these strange things, it could cause bad feeling as some of the women are bound to be jealous. I'm also concerned they might think I'm getting preferential treatment again. It's really not worth the hassle, Sal. I know and you know and that's all that matters, I might tell Bea and Jess but that's it.

CHAPTER: THIRTY-SIX

I can't believe over a week has passed since my day out with Alf, it still feels like yesterday. Sal left home hours ago, she's meeting up with Mattie at the community hall and then they are going to the market. I just fancy a day at home on my own.

I can hear Jess shouting for me, now she's frantically banging on my door, she sounds hysterical. I quickly open the door: *"What the hell's going on, calm down and talk to me."*

"Sal's in serious trouble, Bea told me to come and get you. We have got to get to the community hall as soon as possible. Allie we have to go now!"

I'm starting to get a real bad feeling in the pit of my stomach. As soon as we are on our way, I say: *"Tell me everything you know? Like, where is Sal?"*

Jess starts to explain what she knows as fast as she can: *"Bea and I were at the market when we heard Mattie screaming for help. She was running as fast as she could towards us. She was in a right state, practically incoherent. From what we could gather Sal had arranged to meet Mattie at the community hall. She said they were just sitting on the edge of the platform, minding their own business, when Tori, Florence, Nina, and Andrea walked in, and you know what nasty bastards they are! They seemed to be looking for trouble, Tori was really pissed-off about something, so the other women who were there left as quickly as they could. She and Sal went to leave but they wouldn't let Sal go. The four of them blocked the door and told Mattie to get out, but she refused to leave Sal on her own with them.*

Christ, Allie, she's out to get Sal. She's the youngest of all of us and Mattie's not much older. Apparently, it's because the evil cow knows about your day out with Alf. Someone must have overheard Sal telling Mattie and whoever that bitch was told Tori. Mattie said Tori kept screaming at Sal saying that it was all bullshit and you are nothing but a fucking fantasist and a lying bitch.

When Sal tried to defend you and convince her it was the truth, she started slapping her around the face, saying the trouble with you is; it's always Allie this and Allie that, well, she's not here to protect you now. That's when Mattie said both she and Sal tried to stand up to them and that's when it turned really nasty.

Mattie then said Tori, started giving Sal a beating and before she could help her; the other three started slapping and pushing her around. Then they physically threw her out of the community hall and told her to fuck off. As soon as she got outside she saw all the Jeeps had gone, including theirs, so she started running as fast as she could towards the market, screaming for help. Bea heard her before she saw her. As soon as she had told Bea what was going on, Bea told me to get you and then go straight to the community hall."

"Is Mattie OK?"

"Sameena said she would take her to Dr Jenna's unit as she was inconsolable, she is worried sick about Sal. I turned back to talk to Bea but she had gone. Mattie said, she thinks Tori's taking it out on Sal in order to get at you!"

It feels like the journey to the community hall is taking forever, at last we are finally here. Before Jess stops, I jump out of the Jeep and run straight into the place. I immediately look for Sal, she is curled up on the floor, I can see her face and arms, are bloodied and bruised. Then everything happens so fast. As I turn, I can see Florence, Nina and Tori attacking Bea. Nina is nearest to me, so I grab hold of her as Bea lands one almighty punch to the side of Florence's jaw and she goes straight down. Nina tries to throw a punch at me but I hurl her, as hard as I can, against the nearest wall, she goes down. Bea leaves Tori for me and I do to her what she has done to Sal, plus a bit extra. Andrea heads for the door and Jess trips her up and is just about to kick her when Bea stops her. I then go over to Sal and gently help her to stand; she's holding her arm and is in a lot of pain. The four of us walk out of the community hall - leaving the garbage behind!

....

"They are showing violent tendencies again. This is unacceptable."

"They went to help their friend and then they were defending themselves."

"The four women who instigated this violence need to be isolated from all of the humanoids. They are to be observed more closely as I am not sure if they will be suitable for our needs. I have spoken to the woman called Bea and she has tried to explain to me her reasons for her part in the violence. We know she cannot be part of the Researchers' plans but the women listen to her and she could be useful to us in other ways.

I think you should reconsider interacting with the woman called Allie, as this is not the first time she has resorted to violence. Has she explained to you the reasons for her behaviour?"

"No. She does not need to explain anything to me as I understand her reasons. She was protecting her friend. I

will not be reconsidering interacting with Allie. I have made my choice."

CHAPTER: THIRTY-SEVEN

We have asked Sal, Mattie and Sameena to drive to all the units, the parks, the lake and the market and tell everyone there is to be a meeting in the community hall in an hour and it is compulsory and anyone who doesn't turn up will be dragged there. Needless to say, I'm still well and truly pissed-off. Partly due to what happened to Sal, partly because I feel guilty.

Everyone has finally turned up; not everyone is here by choice, but they are here. All the women are seated but not a sound can be heard, I'm standing on the raised platform. I don't need to raise my voice as the acoustics in the hall are so good, however, because I am struggling to contain my temper I can hear my voice rising: *"Bea and I have called this meeting as some things have got to be sorted out. What happened recently to Sal cannot be allowed to happen again. If, by chance, someone hasn't heard, Sal was badly beaten up and Mattie was scared half to death. If I thought for one moment putting the perpetrators into the furnace would benefit us all, I would.*

The reason for this meeting is; we need to have some guidelines and penalties. Some amongst us seem to have lost their humanity. Unless we all agree to have guidelines and penalties, we'll end up turning on each other. Bea now wants to talk to you:"

"I've asked Dima for a suggestion box, slips etc, which will be placed in the community hall for the next three days. It really is important that every one of you writes down the guidelines you think we should have and what you think should happen if these guidelines are broken. As soon as Allie and I have gone through your suggestions slips, another meeting will be announced so we can discuss what the majority of you have asked for. We can then decide on what should be chosen as guidelines and what should be chosen as appropriate penalties. Decisions will only be made if there is a majority vote. That's it, this meeting is now over."

I wait for Sal and then we head home. She knows I feel responsible for what happened to her, she's told me I shouldn't; but I do. We have got to make sure these guidelines and penalties work, because, if Tori ever attempts to hurt Sal again; I won't be responsible for my actions.

CHAPTER: THIRTY-EIGHT

I've just collected the suggestion box from the community hall and it's full to the brim. God knows what the women have suggested for guidelines and penalties. Bea's already in my room waiting for me, so we can go through all the suggestions together. As we are reading through what the women do and do not want, I turn to Bea: *"If we make rules of everything in this bloody box, we'll be living in a police state!"*

"That cannot be allowed to happen. We only need enough rules to keep us civilised. Most of the suggestions for guidelines look as though they are asking for more or less the same thing, but nearly all the suggestions for penalties are too severe. I would like five guidelines and five penalties, what do you think?"

"I'm fine with that. I think the majority of the women will accept the guidelines but the penalties will have to be toned down a bit."

"There needs to be a vote after each suggestion and a final decision can only be made if the majority are in favour, do you agree?"

CTJ Reeves: Asmeron

"Yes. A lot of the women are asking if there could be some sort of mediation. I think we should speak to Dr Jenna and see if she will be willing to help. I would like the two of us to do the meeting together."

"What I would suggest is; you should tell them the guidelines that we have chosen and I will follow with the appropriate penalties.

....

It has taken us longer than we thought it would have but we now have our five guidelines and five penalties. We want to get this over and done with so we have asked Sal, Mattie and Sameena to drive to all the units again, the lake, the parks and the market and inform everyone there is to be a meeting in the community hall in an hour.

Bea and I are standing on the platform in the community hall waiting for the women to appear. I'm sure it's been a good hour since Sal, Mattie and Sameena notified everyone. Slowly the women start to appear, it's in dribs and drabs, but they are here, probably more out of curiosity than anything else. Once everyone has sat down and settled down, I clap loudly to get their attention and then I begin:

"Bea and I have carefully looked through all of your suggestion slips and we hope you will agree with us that too many guidelines and too many penalties will be detrimental. Many

of you have stated that, if feasible, you would like there to be some kind of mediation before any actual penalty is imposed in order to try and change the individual's behaviour. Bea and I have spoken to Dr Jenna as she's qualified in human behaviour and she says she would be happy to help. The majority of your suggestions are asking for, more or less, the same things, which can be covered by five guidelines. Each of the penalties you have asked for, Bea and I think are far too severe. We have attempted to modify the suggestions you've made for penalties and there will be a vote taken after each one. I will let you know the guideline that has been chosen and Bea will let you know what we think would be the appropriate penalty. The first one is:

"Respect each other and consider each others' feelings."

I turn to Bea who says:

"If you cannot do this then there will be mediation with Dr Jenna, to try and find the cause and a solution. Ok, let's vote, all those in favour of that one please raise your hands. Great that is unanimous; let's have the next one Allie:"

"No stealing."

"All of your belongings will be taken from you. Again raise your hands if you agree. The majority of you are in favour, so that's carried, number three Allie:"

"No more actual fighting with each other."

"We can't have a repeat of what happened recently, we have all got to live together here. So, if you cannot control yourself there will be a period of mediation. If both Dr Jenna and the person involved feel this has not worked and the violence continues, then Dr Jenna will report this to the android and he will decide on an appropriate penalty."

There appears to be dissent in the room over this one. Judging by the grumblings going on we might not get this passed. To stop the murmuring Bea shouts: *"Ok, Ok, can we please take a vote now:"*

Before any vote can take place Tori stands up: *"Why do we need to involve the android? It's incapable of any feelings so God knows what it will decide as a penalty. Why can't we keep these guidelines and penalties between ourselves?"*

"Most of the suggestions for penalties were an eye for an eye and after what happened to Sal, that's how Allie and I feel, but this is not the right way. The android is against physical violence, so, maybe he can think of something that Allie and I cannot. If one of you can tell us how to deal with this problem, please feel free to raise your hand....as none of you seem to have any suggestions, we are going to vote on this again. So, all those in favour raise your hands now. It looks as though

we have a majority albeit small, this one is carried. Next one Allie:"

"No intimidation or bullying."

"Any occurrence of intimation or bullying should be reported as soon as possible to Dr Jenna, Allie or me. This claim will be investigated, if it is found to be true, mediation will be offered, if this is refused we will have no choice but to involve the android again. All of you in favour please raise your hands. It seems we have a slim majority again but this one is carried. There's only one more left, over to you Allie:"

"No attempting to split up any partnership that has developed between a woman and a particular humanoid. I think they call this pairing."

"You will be ostracised by everyone until a majority vote says otherwise. Ok a show of hands for this one, all those in favour raise your hands. Although there are a few of you who do not agree with this, the vast majority are in favour so this too is carried.

Allie and I would like to thank you for co-operating in this. We honestly believe that having a simple set of rules to live by will make life easier for all of us in the situation we find ourselves. This meeting is now over."

CHAPTER: THIRTY-NINE

I really think that since the meeting all the women are starting to have a better relationship with each other. I've put together another portfolio of my sketches, so I'm taking them down to the market to show on my stall. The women who haven't got, or don't want a stall, are happily helping those who have and co-operation seems to be the word of the day, I just hope it lasts. There are a few humanoids walking around but I can't see Alf amongst them. The atmosphere is good, the women are laughing; it looks like it's going to be a really nice day.

I can see Lorcan approaching Sal's stall, so I'm hoping Alf might be here. She runs over to him, after a few minutes I can see her trying to get Jess's attention, she talks to her and then she comes over to me and says: *"Lorcan has asked me to spend the day with him. Jess is going to help Mattie on the stall. He said to tell you Alf is waiting for you at the unit and would like to see you."*

"Did he say why?"

"No."

Sal runs back to Lorcan and then they both disappear from view. I pack up my stall and head home, where I find Alf standing by my door. He asks me if he can come in, which hasn't happened before. He moves the cubes closer together, and when we are sat opposite each other, he says: **"Allie, do you remember asking me about the Researchers' plans when we were at the Plantation?"**

"Yes."

I said I would explain everything to you. It is important that you listen to everything I say without interruption. Do you agree to do this?"

"Yes."

"It is time you knew everything the Researchers had in mind for the future of the humanoids and human beings. We have the ability to create more androids and humanoids but this is not what the Researchers had planned. Their dream was for a completely new species, a new world, to be populated by the progeny of humans and humanoids. It was necessary for us to rescue you in order to harvest your eggs which will be fertilised using our own DNA which was originally obtained from the Researchers and enhanced to create the humanoids on Asmeron and for those who may follow. These were then cleared of any radiation or abnormality and put into

cryostasis for future use. We also altered your lung capacity in order to help you adjust to the environment on Asmeron and, after the woman you called Grace died of a heart attack, we strengthened your heart capacity also."

What he's saying isn't making sense to me. I'm unable to stay quiet as I need to say something: *"This isn't possible, you're not living beings."*

"Part of the Researchers' project was genetic manipulation to turn off genes that caused severe genetic disorders. During this process they learned how to manufacture synthetic DNA using parts of their own DNA. They used the androids they created to help with this process and after a number of years and a number of failures the first humanoids were born - part human, part machine. Our external appearance slightly differs from each other due to the different manufactured DNA used to create skin, hair colour and height. Whilst our internal structure consists of advanced technology, our appearance is human but we are stronger, faster and far more intelligent than ordinary beings. With the combination of the manufactured DNA and further advanced technology, the Researchers' dream was, with the assistance of genetically modified DNA, all humanoids would develop full consciousness and evolve. To enable humanoids to fully integrate into human life

they wanted a fusion of this synthetic DNA with full human DNA and decided the best way to achieve this would be to impregnate human women. A meeting is to be arranged and everything will be explained to everyone. It is important for all of you to accept what has to be done as this is the only way the human race can survive."

"How do you know whose eggs belong to whom?"

"They have the same code that is inscribed on the device fixed around your neck."

I knew it! I just knew it was a fucking barcode!

"Allie, have you understood everything I have said to you?"

"Oh Yes, I understand alright! Do we get a choice? Don't answer that, I already know the answer will be no. Am I the only one to be told?"

"No. Dima has told Bea."

"What!" "When and why was she told?"

"It was the android's decision. He explained everything to her the day he told her about which countries attacked each other on your planet. Allie, have you understood everything I have said to you?"

"I've understood enough. I want you to leave now!"

CHAPTER: FORTY

What the hell am I supposed to make of what I've just heard? We were rescued, brought to this God forsaken place, given a false sense of security and all they want us for is to be a human incubator for some kind of super, genetically enhanced being.

There's only one person I need to speak to and I need to speak to her right now. I rush headlong to Bea's unit and I'm just about to hammer on the door when it opens and the first thing she says beggars belief: *"I've been waiting for you."*

"You knew why Alf wanted to see me."

"Yes. Sit down Allie. Both of us need to consider this information sensibly before the meeting is held and the women are told."

"Sit down; consider this sensibly; what's wrong with you! How on earth can this information be considered sensibly? Alf said the Researchers wanted a new progeny for a new world, which in reality means, they want to use us to produce a fucking hybrid. Because of the fantasies of some very old

people, we are to be used as lab rats! They removed our eggs when we were unconscious, we have been violated."

"The Researchers' dream was to create a new life form, one that is non-violent, intellectually advanced but free of greed, envy and hate. The humanoids have too little emotion, we have too much. They are extremely rational we can be extremely irrational."

"For God's sake Bea, that sounds all well and good, but after everything you've been through I'm astounded you actually think this is acceptable. I cannot believe you are able to be so blasé about this."

"Was it acceptable that there were enough resources on earth for all human beings, but it was only the minority who lived well whilst the majority died of starvation or did not have enough money to buy the necessities in life? All the money and all the power in the world did not stop egomaniacs from pressing their red buttons!"

"It's still wrong. So you're telling me that you are happy for your eggs to be fertilised with their genetically modified DNA, or whatever else the Researchers did to it, knowing a life will be created, but not knowing if that life will survive or what it will become?"

"If it was possible for me to do this, I would. I believe it is the right thing to do as there is no other way for the human race to *survive, but it won't happen to me and this is not by choice. Remember I told you about being in prison and being tortured. They were terrified I would survive or another government would grant a political amnesty for prisoners. If they had killed me, I would have become a martyr, so they tried one more thing to destroy me - they gave me their version of a hysterectomy."*

"What they did to you Bea was wrong, but it doesn't make what the humanoids want to do to us, right. Apart from being morally wrong, this could be very dangerous. It could result in miscarriages, some of us, maybe all of us, might not survive!"

"We have to survive; otherwise all trace of the human race will cease to exist."

The silence between us is becoming really uncomfortable, so I stand up and walk out. My head is spinning, part of me thinks what Bea has said makes some sort of sense; another part of me wants nothing to do with any of it. Who am I kidding? As if we are going to be given a choice? When I get back to my unit I'm still as confused as ever, I'm just pleased Sal's not here. God knows how the women will react when they find out. I go and lie on my bed, curl up into the foetal position and cry myself dry.

CHAPTER: FORTY-ONE

Dima has informed Bea there is to be a meeting in the community hall and everyone is to be there within the hour and no later. This must be it - everything is about to change. Sal, Mattie and Sameena have again volunteered to drive around and tell everyone about the meeting. This time, as soon as the women have been given the information, they rush to the community hall. They have been summoned by Dima and no-one will defy him; although I'm not so sure about Bea. We haven't been here long, but some of the women are starting to get restless. God knows how they will react when they are told they are to be impregnated. Dima and Alf have just walked into the community hall, I immediately look at Bea but she isn't giving any sign that she knows what's about to be said.

Dima and Alf walk straight to the platform, then turn and face us. I'm bracing myself for what's to come. I can't get my own head around the Researchers' plans so I've no idea how the women will react.

Dima signals for silence and then addresses us all:

"We all have to leave Asmeron immediately."

Momentarily we all become motionless, open-mouthed and mute. Then, instantaneously, there is complete and utter chaos. Everyone is starting to panic and shout out in a cacophony of sound:

"No."

"Why?"

"What's happened?"

"I don't want to leave Asmeron?"

"Why do we have to leave here?"

"What's going to happen to us now?"

"Where the hell are we going to go?"

In a forceful voice Dima says: **"Quiet – I demand silence!"**

Instantly, there is silence. Bea then says to Dima: *"Why do we have to leave?"*

I swear I can see a change in his demeanour. He composes himself and says: **"We frequently monitor both the areas on Asmeron that are not accessible to us. There has been an increase in seismic activity underneath the frozen zone. Our data shows that there have been numerous small ice quakes occurring within the ice sheet itself indicating we have a sub-glacial stratovolcano. Our** *analysis also shows that an eruption is imminent. This eruption will release a thousand times more energy than a normal earthquake and will be of such a scale it will engulf this whole planet in burning magma. The air will become toxic and Asmeron will be immersed in acidic water and thus uninhabitable. We have to leave Asmeron."*

Sal, Mattie and Sameena speak at the same time: *"Have we got time to collect our belongings?"*

Dima refuses to answer, so Alf takes over: *"We calculated there was enough time to load everything we considered a necessity onto our interstellar crafts, this included clearing your units as everything will be needed at a later date. Another interstellar craft is now waiting to take us all away from here, we need to leave Asmeron immediately; time is now against us.*

As soon as Alf has finished talking, they both stride out of the community hall and humanoids appear and start ushering us out of the building. I'm still looking out of the window as the sky has morphed into a murky mix with large quantities of ash floating in the sky. Suddenly, in the distance, I can hear a succession of explosions and the entire community hall begins to shake. Please God, don't let it be happening again! Within seconds the community hall stabilises and the sounds of the explosions diminish. Now we are all panicking and rushing to get outside, without any prior warning, the ground starts to violently shake and then a deafening sound is heard. This must be it– the stratovolcano or whatever it's called has erupted!

I don't even know what should be freaking me out the most, being impregnated with a hybrid or drowning!

Outside the community hall there are two trucks waiting for us. We instantly and frantically climb into the trucks, the temperature is dramatically increasing and I can feel the sweat start seeping from my skin as clouds of steam roil across the sky. As this steam descends it creates severe humidity making it difficult to breath and visibility becomes poor. The lower the steam descends the temperature rapidly drops and the sweat starts to freeze on my body and I now find I'm shivering as it becomes brutally cold.

We accelerate towards the cargo hold of the interstellar craft as ice rain begins to attack us. It feels like burning needles as this acidic rain punctures my clothing and attacks my cold skin. As I become convinced I'm about to die, the trucks drive straight into the cargo hold of the craft. It has only taken us five, at most, ten minutes to get here and my clothing is already in tatters. I'm soaked to the skin and have small burns all over my arms, legs and face. I'm covered in the dirty grey ash that is falling like a deluge from the sky.

The two trucks deposit us all in the middle of an immense cargo hold and then disappear. As my senses return, I start to take in my surroundings. What I can see is a multitude of pods or capsules all around me and seventy-seven dishevelled women are standing in the middle of the cargo hold, of which I am one. Also like me, they are shivering, covered in ash, dripping wet, in pain and terrified.

I can still hear the sound of the volcano from within the craft but now the vibrations I can feel seem to be coming from inside the craft itself. We have taken off, we are airborne and I hope to God, we are not too late!

CHAPTER: FORTY-TWO

Humanoids start to re-appear and as they file in each one stands next to one of these capsule things. Soon after, Dima makes an appearance but Alf is nowhere to be seen. Oblivious to our physical condition, Dima stops, stands in front of us, and says: **"There is no need for concern. When we transported you from Earth to Asmeron this is the method we used. Once the capsule is sealed your bodies will be cleansed, your nutrition and hydration implants adjusted and a strong sedative will be used to place you into suspended animation for the duration of our journey. You are all to remove your clothing and then each one of you is to lie down in a capsule."**

One by one, we apprehensively remove what's left of our clothing and start to slowly walk towards the capsules. This is when some of the women start to become hysterical; others are just rigid with fright. When we were all transported in these glass coffins before, we were oblivious to everything that was happening to us. Now, like me, the women are beyond fear. Whilst, the humanoids are trying to calm down these women and get them to lie down in one of these coffins the rest of us, who are still able to function, continue slowly walking towards the remaining capsules where we just perch on the end of one of these things, forcing ourselves to just focus on the other women. As soon as someone has calmed down and is placed into a capsule, a humanoid slides his hand over a control panel on the lower half of the casing, immediately the upper half descends to close and seal the capsule giving it a transparent egg-like appearance. The next thing that happens is a blue vapour fills the capsule and then rapidly disappears to be replaced by a soft amber glow that stays. As soon as this process is completed the humanoids move on to the next group of women.

One by one the capsules are sealed and now it looks like it's my turn. I can see the amber glow from the capsule next to me and I'm absolutely petrified of being sealed into this coffin. I take a deep breath; close my eyes and lie down, preparing myself for what's to come. I'm sure I can hear my name being called; I open my eyes and see Alf leaning over me. He bends closer and then whispers gently into my ear: **"Allie - The jigsaw puzzle is now complete. The planet we are going to is Earth."**

Then he kisses me!

Alf walks away - my capsule seals - I'm going home!

Printed in Great Britain
by Amazon